MATTHEW COLE LEVINE

The Laws of Inheritance

Monday

I wake on a Monday in June, sweat pooled in the crevasse between the small of my back and a musty white T-shirt, feeling odd. Not quite right. It's my stomach. There's a throbbing in my gut, slight but incessant. Not enough to wake me, but enough to demand my attention in the first blinking moments of the day. Before I even sense the sun I'm shaken by discomfort, my legs feel heavy as pillars and the space between my temples flares. But mostly it's the bellows in my stomach, rising and falling with thunderous huffs, blowing toxic soot into my body.

I shut my eyes, clench my fists, and heave my legs up under me, thinking (because even my logic is weakened) that the mere exertion will right my physiological wrongs. But, I should have seen it coming, it only makes it worse. As my knees slide across linens and my legs swing into open air, the vicegrip clamped around my innards tightens catastrophically.

At this point, I'm not thinking about my father. My mind is concerned only with the agony swimming in my gut. My bare feet make contact with the cold-slab hardwood; my toes curl and my stomach tightens, fighting the fist inside of it. The outside world introduces itself, trying to claw through the pain: one solitary bird chirping in the sunshine, sounding a little *too* happy I think; an engine idling somewhere, lazy in the summer haze.

It's not until I'm at the bathroom mirror—after an arduous two-minute shuffle, during which my stomach begins to tame itself—that my father occurs to me. The toothpaste is tumbling from my lips, a rabid froth, and I peer into my irises and wonder why they look so dull, and I think of him. The man I never met. The man I feel I should love, have some kind of kinship with, even though he died eight months before I was born. I've seen him in faded photographs, dates imprinted on plastic snapshots, and heard a story or two—the Gulf War hero whose valiant future was cut so unceremoniously short.

Sad story, yes—but that's not why I'm thinking of him now. It's something else my mother said during one of the rare moments when she speaks of him, whenever the loneliness becomes too much for her or my badgering breaks down her defenses. He was so young when he died, she would say, her eyes releasing liquid and focusing on nothing. Exactly twenty-five years old, to the day. He would have been a great father.

By this time I've sputtered out the toothpaste and wavered in the shower and dressed myself in something resembling adult clothing, a pair of black jeans with only two small stains on them and a white collared shirt missing a button. The throbbing in my stomach has completely left my mind, superseded now by a trickier concern.

On his twenty-fifth birthday, I say to myself in the kitchen as I pour a heap of cereal up to the brim. The bowl is tangerine-colored and radiates warmth as the sunlight hits it.

On his twenty-fifth birthday from a genetic condition. That's all my mother has told me, and even this nugget of information was gleaned only after an hour of protest, I'm his *son* and I have a *right* to know what *happened* to him. I was fourteen years old at the time I pried this information from her, and by that point I had figured out my fatherlessness was peculiar; the coddling tone of my teachers and the cruel, sneering jokes of fellow middle-schoolers had made it unavoidable. My pleas and protests shook my mother's armor, but only slightly. It was some kind of hereditary gastric disease, she had let slip before her battalions reassembled, turning her cold and distant. "What do you want me to say?" she had finished with a sigh. "He didn't expect it. I sure as hell didn't. But it happened. So what do you want me to say?"

The number 10 bus picks up two blocks away, at Frederick and Yale, meaning I have four minutes now to hurl sugary milk down the sink and grab my backpack and race out the door. Right foot slams the door closed behind me, right hand fumbling with stubborn keys. I bound down the sidewalk, boots clomping in the ninety-degree heat, feeling that pain in my stomach again, irritable little fucker knocking from the inside. I jog down the Baltimore sidewalks. Luckily, after taking the bus nearly every day for as long as I can remember, I know by now that this bus will be two minutes late at least, it's been fighting with that mid-morning traffic downtown. Sure enough, it's only chugging up to the intersection at 10:17, by which point I'm standing conspicuous at the bus stop, seven sweaty quarters clutched between my fingers.

The bus lurches forward before I find a seat, but I right myself and stumble onto some paisley orange fabric, pretending my sideways descent is intentional. I rummage through my bag, feeling outworn paper between my fingertips, and pull a book onto my lap, Kafka's *Metamorphosis*, second reading. For some reason I've had the impulse to pick it up again. *He felt a slight itching up on top of his belly,* I read, *and wanted to touch the spot with one of his legs but immediately pulled it back, for the contact sent a cold shiver through him.*

But my eyes and brain can't focus on the words, not today. The pages are spread open and my fingers trace the lines like Braille, but I raise my head and my vision becomes cloudy. It barely notices the flags and lawn signs passing by the bus windows, which have become more vehement as of late: pro or anti, right- or left-wing, promising a civil war. The presidential election is upcoming, and both sides have become more militant. Violence is imminent and, according to both sides, justified.

Even this means little to me today. I can only think of my dad on his twenty-fifth birthday. Was he thinking of me during his final hours, envisioning what kind of father he might have been?

The little bastard in my stomach, hearing this question uttered by my inner voice, scrapes its talons down the wall of my gut, creating an awful pain that causes me to groan in my bus seat. It's gone within a minute, thankfully, but still there's a scowl on my face. This is a pain I've never felt before, it's unnatural. And—here's the kicker, the thing that's *really* been tormenting me—it is exactly four days before my own twenty-fifth birthday, that quarter-century milestone at which my father met his fate.

The bus rumbles down Frederick Avenue, past chain-link fences and grand old cemeteries, through neighborhoods with starkly different demeanors—a visual spectrum of poverty and wealth drawn on scarred streets and centuries of architecture. It's a long bus ride to work, nearly an hour. Still, all I can do is think.

I arrive at CGT Video Services nearly on time. We're on the

outer fringes of the city at this point, liquor stores and Volvo dealerships abutting each other. My workplace is a squat brick building that looks like a cross between a garage and a motel, but the environs inside are surprisingly pleasant: squares of thick carpeting, the flicker of projectors both analog and digital, old movie posters and memorabilia lining the walls. I pass a few coworkers on the route to my desk, offering a nod and a quick hello, but most of them have their eyes trained on a screen, observing someone else's home movies. This is a job tailor-made for introverts. I could call a few of them friends, but our social hours are usually spent with solitary pleasures, movies and books foremost among them.

My workstation is a study in technology through the years, a looming Mac surrounded by old tape decks and projectors. Visions and memories are cluttered on my desk, taking the form of film reels, tiny USB drives, obsolete videotapes, and fragile DVDs. Currently I'm in the process of transferring a family's home movies from faded celluloid into the digital realm, an undertaking which comprises about ninety percent of our work here.

"Hey Darren," says someone as they pass by my desk. I look up and see Shannon smiling in my direction, eyes gleaming. She's older than I am, about thirty, and has an air of disarming sincerity about her; she could turn a conversation about the weather into an earnest heart-to-heart. But she keeps on walking, carrying a coffee mug to her station before I have the chance to think of a charming response. Anyway, both of us might be happier with this fumbling, unspoken attraction; anything more than that comes dangerously close to real human interaction.

I spool one of the 8mm reels onto a projector, fitting minuscule plastic nibs into the brittle sprocket holes. An orgy of cables and wires stretches from the projector through a massive converter and into the rear of the Mac—chemicals and light becoming ones and zeros. The images now flickering on my screen, drunkenly appearing after a slight delay, involve an old man seated at a long table, birthday cake ablaze in front of him, seemingly hundreds of candles dripping wax onto frosting. His family surrounds him, three or four generations singing and applauding as he musters the breath to blow out the candles. It's nearly dusk and the red-orange lighting, dancing in the grain of the film stock, lends the footage an appropriate mystery, turning it both more real and more dreamlike.

The old man blows out the candles in a prolonged breath. He smiles, leans back in his chair, eyes glassy but full of joy. Next to him, a blond girl of about five or six clutches at his arm, grinning—she's missing two front teeth. There must be eighty years between them.

* * *

The unbearable pain has settled, mostly, into a dull and constant ache, dormant beneath the skin. I can tolerate it for the most part, though adjusting in my chair has become a masochistic exercise.

Only twice today did I have to flee to the bathroom, hand trembling over my stomach as I hobbled down the hallway. Gasping, I lifted my T-shirt above my chest and peered at my torso, trying to identify the area where something festered and fumed inside. The piercing electric light made my skin look lifeless, a pale color much unlike its usual shade of brown, inherited from my Black father and my white mother; I'm frequently self-conscious about the lightness of my skin, but today especially so and for entirely different reasons. Prodding gingerly at my body, I was *sure* I felt something—a hard protuberance, my flesh transforming. But both times I forced myself to breathe in deeply, and though my sides throbbed in response, I was able to go on with my day as though everything were ordinary.

The bus ride home takes me seventy minutes—fewer than on many other nights. *Metamorphosis* is spread open in front of me, Gregor Samsa is acclimating to his new form, but the words just seem like empty shapes, abstract figures on a blank canvas. My brain is preoccupied with the concept of twenty-five years, the meaninglessness of that stretch of time. These years represent the blink of an eye when placed along some grand cosmic timeline, but also constitute, I think to myself, an infinity of moments and decisions. I cannot imagine my life continuing for two or three times as long as it already has.

During this musing, my eyes roam blankly. Now and then I catch the gaze of the other passengers—three young Black women eyeing me from the back of the bus, a middle-aged white man clutching his briefcase on his lap. I wonder what they think of me; are they focused on my skin color, trying to fit it into a neat category, or are they equipped with some kind of X-ray vision to detect my internal unease? Maybe they aren't thinking about me at all.

I'm used to the scrutiny, this feeling of in-betweenness. When my father died, his life insurance payout allowed me and my mom to live comfortably for a while. I grew up in West Baltimore near Tremont, where liquor stores and security-gated church ministries started to give way to wide streets and well-manicured parks. Suburbia loomed to the west, Shipley

Hill and Lexington to the east. I was pulled in two different directions, unsure of who I was or wanted to be and given no guidance—not by my teachers, underpaid and overworked, more concerned with the students who posed an immediate threat (to themselves and others); and not by my mother, who within a couple of years was forced to work two jobs to provide for us. Would it have been any easier with a father figure around? It seemed too simple; how could the mere presence of another man have helped me understand myself?

The bus drops me off at Frederick and Yale shortly after nine. I wince in pain as my body contorts itself onto the sidewalk, but then I remember I haven't eaten all day—maybe this is a new, more explicable kind of anguish.

Summer has arrived; dusk is settling in. The reddening sky teems with the thrill of a humid night, the trees shudder at the touch of a warm breeze. I walk two blocks north and half a block to the east, where the yards are tiny and the streets narrow but the stately old homes carry a modest elegance. Many of my neighbors are out enjoying the weather, conversing on front steps or hosing down their gardens. Faces every shade of color nod in my direction—my favorite thing about the neighborhood I live in, the simple, undramatic fact of its diversity. My uniquely colored skin, green-brown eyes, and curly hair seem to symbolize that pluralism.

The brief jaunt home from the bus stop has fatigued me, and as I thrust open the front door, toss my bag onto hardwood, and collapse on the poorly-cushioned couch, I realize that every last ounce of my energy has been spent.

My mind continues to wander, though, mostly toward the past. My inability to find an anchor for my identity was not for lack of trying. Middle-school years were spent with sports: hand-me-down baseball gloves and soccer pads and football helmets, halfhearted attempts to bond with other boys, mimicking their wolfpack confidence. But it never fulfilled me and I didn't grow much during puberty, so my athletic career ended before high school. Around that time some of the guys in my neighborhood started gravitating east toward Lexington, where the allure of ground-level drug work—selling caps of low-grade heroin on street corners, acting as gopher and hired gun for men who considered themselves gangsters—was too much to ignore for someone young, without money or a sense of mortality. But I despised this world, more for its crudity than its violence; to me it was the lowest point of zombie capitalism, becoming a slave to the heartless master of money.

My stomach growls. With superhuman effort and a guttural moan, I raise myself from the couch and stumble to the kitchen, kicking off my shoes along the way. Mom has already been home, briefly: there's a note telling me that she bought ingredients for tacos, that I should leave some for her, that I shouldn't wait up because she won't be home til after midnight. Sure enough, they're lined up on the top row of the fridge: thawed beef and crimson tomatoes and fresh lettuce bought from Lexington Market. I don't even know when she had time to buy food for us. She continues to work two jobs: the DMV from eight to four-thirty, south of the city in Glen Burnie; then a 90-minute break before her shift at Kibby's, serving subpar food to a crowd that's only there for the beer. Seventy hours a week, easily. I tell her not to worry about me, I can provide for myself and it's probably time this twenty-four-year-old moved out anyway. But whenever I bring it up she becomes distraught (something she normally hides at all costs) and says she would go mad without my company in the house. She's already lost my father; without me here, she says, it would be hard to find a purpose.

So even though my stomach shudders and moans with each movement, and all I really want is some soup and dry toast, I dutifully cook the meat and dice tomatoes and chop lettuce. Before returning to the couch I Saran-wrap everything, return it to its refrigerated habitat, and leave a note for my mother on the table, scrawling a quick "Thanks Mom, love you."

Flick on the TV in the living room. We only get the major networks—reality shows, empty sitcoms, increasingly dire news reports. But tonight, blessedly, PBS is playing *I Walked with a Zombie*, and I thank some nonexistent god for this temporary diversion.

I force myself to swallow some food, chewing small, uncertain bites, and it plummets down my esophagus and lands with the force of an A-bomb. Shockwaves of pain course through my stomach lining, climbing up the walls with serrated talons. A feral growl comes from within, and I don't know how to describe it but it feels somehow sentient, as though some inner being has resented this intrusion.

I return the taco to its plate. Juices flecked with meat and spices drip down my hand. I figure I'll give my body a rest before attempting another swallow.

The lustrous shadows and monochrome faces on TV are inviting, but still I sink deeper into memory. Maybe my impending birthday has put me in a reflective mood. Sports and crime did nothing for me, they were lives I couldn't take seriously. And while most of my father's family bowed down before the gods of war, viewing the military as some enshrined collective where the brave and loyal achieve their true potential, I couldn't buy in to the usual jingoism. Is it brave to serve as a pawn for an empire that couldn't care less about you, sacrificing you for the idols of money and power? Is it noble to kill a stranger in another land who has been fed the same lies of duty and nationalism? My mom's father fought in Vietnam, my dad's brother in the Gulf War—he served in the navy and never took part in ground combat, unlike my father. They tell me not to dismiss it, the armed forces might be just what I need. *Freedom is at stake*, they say, and it takes all my willpower not to laugh in their faces. Maybe my father died from a genetic condition, but still I feel like the army took him from me. He fought in Iraq, came home, and died five years later. Enough time to bear a son who would soon be set adrift in the world.

I lean forward and take another bite, trying to tame my stomach into submission. This one is more successful than the first, though still I get the sense that molten magma expands and hardens inside me.

All of these wayward years in my youth left me with art as a sole trusted companion. Having been left alone for most of my childhood, I grew accustomed to solitude. Art was the obvious course of action, a refuge for the aimless and disillusioned. I drifted to movies first; the tiny Hollywood Cinema was a short bus ride away in Arbutus, and it was relatively easy to sneak from one theater to the next. I was joined by the only true friend I've ever had, an awkward redhead named Mikey who loved movies even more than I did; most days after school we'd hightail it back to his house and watch old action flicks on his dad's entertainment center, sometimes sneaking beer or whiskey. Mikey moved to New York for college years ago; we haven't talked sense, and I get the feeling that he wants to put his Baltimore roots behind him.

Before long, my tastes turned toward the literary, probably

because books allowed me to retreat further within myself. The Enoch Pratt Library was close by on Edmondson, and by the time I reached high school I would spend most of my time there. A sympathetic librarian started sliding me books she thought I'd like: first *Animal Farm* and *Monster*, then the really troubling stuff, which she recommended in hushed tones as though they were illicit materials—Ralph Ellison, James Baldwin, Camus, Faulkner. I believed in the goodness of people as a literary concept, but it was harder to maintain that faith in reality, especially whenever I felt dirty looks from strangers or spotted an array of blinking police lights around a freshly strewn corpse. Why would I not want to exist in a world where I could shelter and preserve my ideals?

Back in the present, in a dark living room on Massachusetts Avenue, there's another wild contortion in my gut. A throb emanates through every nerve ending. Somehow I rise and shuffle to the kitchen and scrape the rest of my food into the trash. This is all I can tolerate today. Before retreating back to the couch, I ball up my fist and punch my stomach three times, hoping to bruise myself as a manifestation of my anger. What the hell is going on inside of me? For the first time, terror mixes with pain.

Tuesday

I wake around 2:30 in the morning, crawl to the bathroom, and vomit blood into the toilet. All I can sense at first is an even sharper pain, so blunt and vicious it throttles me awake; the fireworks going off all over my body prevent me from getting to my feet and walking forward. So hands and knees it is, scuttling over wood floors, and at this point I think I'm still dreaming, one of those nightmares so potent that it inflicts real, physical pain.

I make it to the rim of the toilet just in time, thrust up the seat with sweaty palms, and feel the torrent of blood and bile and whatever hurtling through my esophagus. It lands with a loud, emphatic *plunk* and I can feel moisture, a thick sort of water, splash back at me and land on my forearm, which is resting against cold, white porcelain.

It's not until I reach with my left arm, extending across my body, and switch on the light that I see the deep crimson color staining the bowl in front of me. In my delirium it looks almost beautiful, like one of those insane Italian horror movies from the '70s. But my brain is catching up with me and begins to fathom that this blood and strange, viscous substance have just come from inside me. My nerves are connecting, the loop is closing, and now I can feel the pain in my stomach once again. It pulsates slowly, like an oscillating fan whose blades are exposed inside my gut.

I sit there for three minutes, though it feels ten times longer. I finally work up the courage to flush the toilet and tear off a scrap of toilet paper to dry the splatter of blood. Using the rim of the toilet as a crutch, I bring myself to my feet and wobble there meekly, positive I'm about to collapse to the floor. But somehow I stay standing, turn off the light, and shuffle back to bed, my body feeling wrecked and ravaged from the inside.

I lie there for a few minutes hoping sleep will return to me, but there's no chance. I realize now that I'm shaking—not a constant shiver, but a periodic tremor that ebbs and flows.

Groaning, I lean over the side of the bed and pick up a decrepit old laptop. I open the screen and stare at it blankly. What do I hope to find? What kind of answers do I think this piece of technology can offer me?

"Vomiting blood" counts as one of the more disturbing Google searches I've undertaken, but I type out the words and press enter, hands shaking from either pain or fear. A list of disorders stares back at me, the usual suspects: stomach ulcers, esophageal varices, syndromes named after their discoverers. None of these seem quite right, though; none of them, for example, list as a symptom a fleshy protuberance in the middle of the abdomen.

I do one last search before I shut the laptop, my fingers dancing of their own accord. I don't even know why this comes to mind. But I type out the words anyway: "Gulf War syndrome." I've heard the condition talked about; I remember it uttered in fearsome news reports from when I was a child. This would have been the early 2000s, around the time of Uncle Sam's second jaunt to Iraq, and some of the newscasters' alarming tones carried an implicit warning: *don't you remember what happened last time?*

"A cluster of medically unexplained chronic symptoms," reads one website, "that can include fatigue, headaches, joint pain, indigestion, insomnia . . ." The list of symptoms goes on. "Functional gastrointestinal disorders" are listed here, too, though the cause for such maladies has not yet been determined and the VA "continues to conduct research." Agitated by my restless body, my mind races in every direction. It can't have been a coincidence, I tell myself as I lie in bed, sweating: my father returns home from Iraq and dies a few years later from a condition he didn't even know he had.

But what does that have to do with me? What kind of disease have I inherited?

I fall asleep at some point, around the time the skies begin to pale and some bird whistles sharply at the new day. My state of mind between five and seven a.m. is unreadable, churning grotesquely. Nightmares unfurl before I even fall asleep, wild fantasies of illness and conspiracy, and maybe it's my fatigue and disorientation but these scenarios don't seem farfetched to me.

Two hours after my brain sends me into a violent sleep, my alarm goes off. Twinkling digital bells stab into my eardrum. Maybe it's the pounding in my head and the general feeling of numbness, but my stomach actually feels better—in a state of dormancy, perhaps.

For a good ten minutes I lie there, debating whether I should be responsible and go to work, haul myself to the hospital, or continue hibernating in my sweaty twin-sized bed, hoping everything will work itself out. But my employers aren't exactly forgiving of sick days, and in any case I'm not on my mother's health insurance and have none of my own, and neither of us has the funds to drop a couple thousand on hospital bills. Maybe, I try to convince myself, a little distraction might be just what I need to get my mind right. So I force myself to begin the day, kickstarting my body into action like it's a rusty lawnmower.

Step one: brush my teeth. I teeter to the bathroom, legs shaking. Mouth full of foam, hands barely strong enough to elevate my toothbrush. I half expect, when I spit into the sink, that blood and bile will be mixed in with the chemical froth, but no—it's just good old toothpaste.

Step two: stand under the shower and make myself appear non-zombie-like. I rock beneath the spray of water, suffering from that all-consuming fatigue that clouds your head and torments your muscles after only a few hours of sleep. The shower feels almost strong enough to knock me over, but I muster the strength to lather shampoo and run a bar of soap across my fragile body.

I grab a piece of dry toast before stumbling out the door—figuring I should stuff *something* into my belly—and shuffle four blocks to the bus stop at Frederick and Yale. This part of my routine is muscle memory by now, which is fortunate because I'm not even aware of my surroundings today. I bump into a bitter old man on the way, and I can barely notice him glare at me from beneath silver-colored eyebrows, muttering.

The bus pulls away just as I reach the corner, turning left down Yale. I utter a low and somber "fuck," and a woman with a large purse squints at me. I collapse onto concrete steps to wait twenty minutes for the next bus, obstructing somebody's narrow front walkway, and don't have the energy to pull out a book or observe the world around me—I simply rest my head in my hands and take up space, breathing laboriously.

I'm late for work, about forty-five minutes, though I doubt anyone even notices when I trudge inside. I make a beeline for my desk, barely able to lift my feet, and throw my bag onto the laminate surface with a miserable groan. With increasing frequency I'm aware of a persistent throb in my stomach, the simultaneous aches in my head and gut duking it out for supremacy.

Shannon stops by my cube around noon, fingers hooked through an old coffee mug, her nails painted a bright magenta. Her hair is in a tight ponytail and she wears a trace of lipstick. The lights overhead are pale and buzzing, and I have a momentary awareness of how pathetic I must appear.

"Hey," she says, taken aback.

"Hi."

"You look terrible." There's no meanness in her voice, only a touch of empathy. "No offense."

"I know I do." I pause the video playing on my monitor, which has been torture to watch for the last half-hour; I feel I need some Dramamine, made seasick by the constant motion. "Didn't get much sleep last night."

"Is everything alright?"

"Yeah," I mutter, shrugging. "I mean, not currently, but I'm fine."

She taps the ceramic mug, fingernails clacking. "I was gonna ask if you want to see a movie tonight. *The Fly* is playing at the Charles."

"Shit. Original or remake?"

"The original," she says with a weak smile. Then she adopts a high-pitched voice and leans over my cubicle wall, imitating the man-fly caught in a spider's web: *"Help me, help me . . ."*

I groan, shift in my chair, and glance up at Shannon. "Any

night but tonight, really."

"No problem." She squints at me before stepping away, and her blue eyes glimmer. "You sure you're okay?"

"Yeah, I—"

I never finish my sentence. Instead, feeling another wave of pain, I plant my hands against the plastic arms of the rolling chair, jettison myself upward, round the corner of my cubicle wall, and brush past her toward the bathroom, where I collapse in front of the toilet just in time, knees slamming against the tile floor. I'm sure she can hear the sounds of my retching outside the bathroom door; they can probably hear it in Virginia, some fisherman detecting an awful sound as it echoes over the waves of the Atlantic.

I emerge about two minutes later, after splashing my face with cold water (an attempt at rejuvenation that fails miserably) and gargling tap water. I even consider squeezing some pinkish handsoap into my mouth to wash out the taste. There's no blood involved this time, thankfully—only a thick, clear liquid that looks like ectoplasm.

Shannon talks me into going to the hospital—she says she won't take no for an answer. I claim that it's just some stomach bug, hardly convincing myself; and I give the usual excuses, I'm broke as fuck and don't have health insurance. But even while I'm saying the words, Shannon places a hand lightly on my back and steers me out of the building. We shuffle across the parking lot to Shannon's red Honda, into which I collapse, feet brushing aside empty soda cans. The pain in my stomach has begun to win its battle against the throb in my temples and roars victoriously.

Priority Care Clinics is in a dreary brick building by the side of the highway, where it seems a strip mall should be standing instead. Somehow I make my way through the sliding glass doors, Shannon at my side. I tell myself that I need to repay her for her kindness, in ways I don't know how.

She grabs the forms and brings them to me as I writhe in a chair made of stiff fabric. A painting of a cove with a lighthouse at dusk looms on the wall above me. The waiting room is nearly empty at one in the afternoon on a Tuesday, save for a weary-looking mother and her young daughter hacking up a lung. I squint at the words on the check-in forms, the clipboard resting against my knees, and fill out everything the best I can. Next to the question about my family's medical history, I don't know exactly what to write: "genetic stomach condition – father" is the best I can come up with, and it reminds me of the mysteries I've been able to shut out of mind until now, the unspoken traumas that linger in my rearview.

Fifteen minutes later, I'm sitting on a sheet of starched paper, taming the wrath inside me, glancing at everything in the room—a calendar, a stuffed animal in the shape of a dragon, a perfectly round clock whose second hand ticks interminably. The smell is sharp like ammonia, worsening my nausea. I glance at Shannon, who sits in a small plastic chair against the wall.

"Shannon . . . thanks for bringing me, but you don't have to stay, really."

"How are you gonna get back?" I shrug and swallow roughly. "Don't worry. This means I get out of work, anyway."

I laugh and experience a brand new pain as my insides rattle from the effort. "I owe you."

"Yeah you do." She grins at me again. Why couldn't this conversation have happened weeks ago, when I wasn't a pathetic shell of a man hunched over on a hospital bed? Regardless, I feel the need to perform pleasant company, attempting a conversation.

"So . . ." I moan as a preamble. "When you're not spying on other people's home movies, what do you do?"

She ponders for a moment. "Try to amuse myself. I don't know. I like swing dancing."

"Really?" I try to picture her in a flapper gown, ricocheting across a dance floor. This mental image completes the hazy, half-formed vision I had of Shannon before now, filling in the colors of her portrait in my brain. "Swing dancing?"

"Yeah." She smiles to herself and looks away. "I studied dance in school for a couple years. Ballet and interpretive and all that. But swing was always my favorite. Now I just do it for myself."

"That's good. Nothing wrong with that."

"Yeah . . ."

There's a long silence. It seems she wants to say something else, something uncomfortable; I get the sense that she's been waiting for a conversation like this, a chance to give voice to the things in her life she wishes she could change.

"Why'd you leave school?" I finally ask, encouraging her to go on.

"I had to drop out when my mom got sick." She says it slow and hesitant. "Lung cancer. We couldn't afford an at-home nurse, so I've been taking care of her a lot."

"I'm sorry." I try to think of something else to say, something that doesn't sound hollow and forced. I wonder how much I should reveal of my family's own skeletons, a subject I've broached with almost nobody.

But before I allow my emotional armor to crumble, the door bursts open and a doctor walks in. Dr. Carstens is her name, tall and with a steady, rapid-fire way of speaking that's kind and assertive at once. She smiles gravely as she asks about my discomfort and requests that I lift my shirt. Her fingers prod at my flesh, firm yet careful, and they linger at a certain area near the center of my abdomen, where I can feel something small and cartilaginous give resistance. I can't help but squeal in pain, a horrible grimace etched onto my features.

My temperature is taken—102, the thermometer reads, and I wonder if that's from lack of sleep or something else—and my blood pressure, too. Then she brings up the subject I've been dreading in a manner that seems shockingly casual to my withered mind.

"Darren, you indicated that your family has a history of stomach problems. Can you tell me more about that?"

"Not much. All I know is my dad died from a stomach condition when he was twenty-five."

"Mmm," she mutters, hiding any trace of emotion. "Do you know what the condition was?"

I exhale slowly. "No. He died before I was born. My mom hasn't told me much . . ."

"Could you ask her, please, and let me know? That affects things, of course. We need as much information as possible."

"I can try. She doesn't like talking about it. And what she *has* told me I practically had to force out of her."

Dr. Carstens gives a brusque nod and shuffles her feet. "I understand, but she might feel differently when she learns that your health is at stake. Talk to her, please, and call me back as soon as you can."

In the meantime, she says, we'll take some X-rays and see what we can find. She grabs me lightly by the elbow and helps me to my unsteady feet. I'm taken to the X-ray room and strapped with a thick lead vest, and even in my pain I'm dreading the hospital bill that will arrive in the near future, the price of self-preservation.

After the X-rays are taken, I'm ushered back to the hospital room, where Shannon and I are left waiting for the images to develop. That same silence returns, not just awkward now but weighted with the specter of mortality. Almost inadvertently, we've both laid out our families' hardships, despite the fact that we were practically strangers a few hours ago.

"I'm sorry to hear about your dad," she says, breaking the silence.

"Yeah. I've seen him in pictures and home movies and stuff," I say in halting words, feeling the need to divulge something. "But when I think of him, there's no mental image. Just some gray shadow I feel like I should care about." Another long pause. The dull throb returns, hammering a beat in my abdomen. "Sometimes I wonder what I'd be like if he had been around. If I would have turned out differently."

Shannon nods. "I've wondered that too. My dad left a long time ago." She trails off, swallowing hard. "It makes you think about *why* you are the way you are. The million little things that happened a certain way to give you a personality, your dreams, your fears. If they happened differently, would you be a totally different person? I don't know. There's no use speculating about the kind of people we *could* be." A glimmer of a smile returns. "Time for confession, I guess."

I look at the bland surroundings, the grim sterility of the hospital room. "As good a place as any," I say. Then take a painful breath before asking the next question. "Shannon, I don't want to sound ungrateful, but why are you doing this for me? Don't get me wrong, you're restoring my faith in humanity, but . . . we barely know each other."

She smirks and shrugs again, an endearing gesture, and I

wonder if she even knows she's doing it. "Morbid curiosity." But then she answers truthfully, and there's that same generosity in her voice. "Do you remember the conversation we had your first day at work? Barely even a conversation, really. I asked you why you wanted to work there, just transferring people's home movies all day. Do you remember what you said?"

I nod, touched that she remembers, though now, in retrospect, embarrassed by my response.

"I said I wanted to understand how a normal person lives."

"Just a joke, I know. But the kind of joke that's really an honest answer."

I offer another laugh, which I'm starting to realize is ill-advised as it sends a torrent of pain ballooning through my torso. I open my mouth to offer a pithy response, but then Dr. Carstens returns with the X-rays, two plastic sheets wavering in her hands with a thunderous tremor. She flips on a lightbox and hangs them up, stating in what sounds like optimistic tones that we may have found the reason for my distress. She points at a small, hazy black mass directly in the center of my abdomen, square in my stomach. About the size of a dime with blurry contours, it looks like the wispy evidence of a ghost in some spooky photograph of a haunted house. She rattles off possible explanations: severe indigestion or (more likely, given the symptoms) a bad ulcer. The small mass beneath the surface of the skin, the doctor concludes, is probably nothing more than a benign cyst or lipoma—both of which are harmless.

"But," she sternly reminds me, "all of this could change when we find out what happened to your father. Ask your mom. Get all the info you can. I'll do some digging too. Can you tell me his name?"

Bryan Trevor, I tell her. She steps to a desk and scribbles down the name, then scrawls out a prescription for lansoprazole. "In the meantime, there's not a lot we can do. Set up an appointment for next week—hopefully the medication will start taking effect by then." She rips off the scrap of paper and hands it to me with what I take to be a pitying look.

Shannon and I lurch through the lobby, stopping by the receptionist's desk, where I make an appointment for the following Wednesday. A small part of me remembers that's five days after my twenty-fifth birthday, and I can't help but wonder if I'll still be around to show up.

We trudge over to the pharmacy and wait while the prescription is filled. I'm hunched in a paisley brown chair, arms folded in front of me. Shannon tries to cheer me up, reciting a quiz from *Cosmopolitan* as the minutes tick by, but eventually she just flips through the pages and reads in silence as I close my eyes to the world.

She drives me home then, passing the narrow but stately rowhomes of Tremont, and drops me off. I give her an apologetic look before I step from the car, a small white bag filled with a vial of pills clutched between my fingers.

"I'm really sorry," I groan. "You haven't seen me at my best."

"Don't apologize." She reaches over and grabs my arm lightly, then pulls her hand away, bashful. "Just feel better. And buy me a drink next week."

"Okay," I say, nodding.

I stumble inside, hearing the churn of Shannon's Honda as it pulls away; drop my bag on the hardwood floor; somehow make it to the kitchen, where I pour half a glass of filtered water (there's no trusting the liquid that comes from the taps these days, it smells like copper and tastes like chemicals); and swallow two immense pills the size of horse tranquilizers. Then back to the sagging couch in the living room, where I collapse and turn on the television—it's just empty light and sound that I'm after, and I'm so exhausted that I don't even turn the channel when the rageful white face of a gun-toting Oath Keeper appears onscreen. My stomach growls and throbs and pounds at the inside of my body. I give my mom a call and leave a message on her voicemail, not expecting her to answer, and vaguely allude to my recent hospital visit. I hang up and remember that I've only had a piece of toast so far today, but I'm not attempting anything else, not now.

* * *

I sleep for the next nine or so hours, my back and limbs contorted in wild positions. My body and mind are completely enervated, as though something alien has sapped my strength. I finally stir shortly after midnight, awakened by the sound of my mom entering the front door, a massive purse slung over her shoulder. She wears a light blue pair of jeans and a red-and-white blouse with a plastic nametag reading "MaryLynn." She kicks the door closed and sighs at once; my eyelids flutter open. Already I can smell the odor of cigarettes clouding around her, mixed with the smell of cheap perfume and two sticks of spearmint gum. She tries to hide her habit from me, but I don't know why. I've told her I would smoke a pack a day if I kept the hours that she does.

Smiling wearily, she pinches the toes on my right foot, which hang over the side of the couch, dangling in a long white sock. I smile back.

"How was work?" I ask, not expecting much of a reply.

"Another day," she grunts and shuffles to the kitchen, discarding her purse and shoes and sliding her stockinged feet over the floor, too tired to lift her legs. From the next room I hear the sound of plates clinking. She pulls a Corona from the fridge, pops the cap from the bottle, and commences making herself a lazy dinner, trying to make those taco ingredients last the whole week. "More importantly, how are you?"

I lie there for a moment, not sure how to answer. I settle on an understatement: "Not great."

"I'm sorry I missed your call," she says, falling into a chair at the kitchen table, fatigue obvious in her voice. "I listened to your message on my way to Kibby's. I could've come home, you know."

I raise myself to a sitting position, body trembling from the effort, and feel my stomach convulse and tighten. I look at my phone on the coffee table: four missed calls from Mom, about every two hours throughout the night.

I shrug in slow-motion. "Not much you could've done. I was just sleeping."

"So, what's going on?" she asks after a pause. "Your stomach?"

Mustering a superhuman amount of willpower, I stand, hobble to the kitchen, and lean against the wall by the doorway. I look at her slouching at the brown-tiled table. She's gotten skinnier over the years, not a healthy, toned thinness but a look of depletion; her shirtsleeves billow around tiny arms and the skin sags from her cheekbones. Despite her typical look of exhaustion, though, my mother is capable of exuding great joy, and on the few instances when she reunites with old friends or sees me truly happy (not a common occurrence, admittedly), she beams and radiates warmth, drawing you closer to her aura.

"Yeah. Started yesterday morning. It's like this constant dull pain—and then, every once in a while, it gets really bad. I just have to curl up and I can't even move. Never felt anything like it."

She narrows her brow and offers a questioning grunt, but as far as I can tell there's no panic in her expression.

"I'm sorry, honey. Maybe it's an ulcer or something? Call in sick tomorrow. Rest up, see what happens. Hopefully it's temporary."

"Maybe."

I suddenly remember my meds, which sit in their plain white bag on the kitchen counter. I pull the bottle from the bag and pop two pills in my mouth, washing the massive capsules down my throat. My stomach grumbles. Mom says nothing, averting her eyes; we've both avoided mentioning the dead elephant in the room.

"It got me thinking about Dad, actually. The doctor wanted me to ask you."

Now the lockdown begins. I can almost hear the warning sirens and clanging metal doors go off in her head. She finishes a taco and leans back in her chair, busying herself with a soggy napkin and resituating her plate on the table. Says nothing.

"I mean, the timing is pretty weird, right? He died when he was twenty-five, on his actual birthday you said, from a stomach condition. And here I am, a few days before I turn twenty-five, suddenly coming down with this . . . I don't know what it is, the worst fucking gut-rot I've ever had—"

"Watch your mouth, please."

"It's scary, though, really. It doesn't feel like an ulcer."

"It's a coincidence, Darren. Don't overreact. Take your meds and see how you feel tomorrow."

I wonder if she's right—maybe my current dismay is more mental than physical. I know that what currently seems like indifference is, in fact, her ongoing grief; I can't blame her for avoiding the subject that intruded violently in her life, turning it tragic. But then I touch my stomach through the fabric of my shirt, two outstretched fingers pressing against it, and I feel something hard and resistant beneath the skin—tiny, the size of a stone, but wholly inexplicable.

"But it *was* a genetic condition, you said. It makes sense to worry about it."

"We had you tested when you were two weeks old," she says, cutting me off, her voice growing terse. "Blood tests and everything. They came back negative."

"Well, what was the disease though? You never even told me—"

"I don't remember, Darren. I didn't even know he had it til after he died, and . . . then I didn't want to hear anything about it."

"What are the symptoms? I mean, was Dad in pain before it happened? Did he see it coming, or was it all of a sudden?"

Her emphatic response consists of shrieking her chair backward, standing with a huff, grabbing her plate, and throwing it in the sink with enough force that it nearly shatters. She tosses her empty bottle in the recycling and grabs another beer from the fridge. At last she returns to the table and collapses on the chair, then leans forward and plants her elbows on the surface. During all this I watch her mutely, my eyes following as she cuts a somber pattern through the room.

"I really don't want to talk about this now," she says finally, almost drained of energy.

I sit across from her at the table before I speak, hoping she'll return my gaze. "No kidding, you never do. But it's important, Mom."

Her eyes close tightly, deepening the wrinkles on her face.

"Part of the reason . . . most of the reason I haven't told you much is 'cause I really don't know anything," she mutters. "He was feeling strange for about a week before. But, Darren, that was completely different. He couldn't move, he couldn't even *breathe* at the end, it hurt him so much. And then he was . . . just gone, okay? It's not some big conspiracy I'm hiding from you. He just died."

It sounds rational enough, and I've never suspected my mother of *lying*, exactly. But still—something seems off, some truths concealed. Maybe it's a gut feeling, I think to myself, then cringe at the gruesome pun.

"How did he never know about this until he was twenty-five? There must have been symptoms before."

She shrugs. "Sometimes these things don't set in 'til adulthood. That's what the doctor told me."

I nod, unsatisfied. Then a question occurs to me. "Who was the doctor?"

My mother sighs, a vehement sound, and I can tell her last remaining shreds of patience are withering away. "What does that possibly matter?"

"I mean, was it a military doctor? He must have gone to the VA hospital, right?"

"Darren . . ." she says, rubbing her temples. For a moment I think that's the end of it, she'll refuse to indulge my sad investigation any further. And I'm ready to accept this and forgive her. But then, to my surprise, she answers. "Yes, it was the Baltimore VA. Some army specialist came in, I don't know, don't ask me to remember his name. He had these surgeons with him. I was scared. I know your dad was. So if they couldn't fix him," she says, opening her eyes, leaning closer, and assuming a pleading tone, "nobody could. Believe that."

Something cynical runs through my mind—*maybe they couldn't fix him because they didn't want to*—but then I wonder if my mom is right about my penchant for conspiracy theories. And anyway, this is the last thing she needs to hear right now. I've weakened her, I can see that clearly. She's worked fifteen hours today and has to wake up in about six.

"I do. Sorry, Mom, I'm just scared. The doctor told me to call her with more information, and . . . I really don't know what to tell her."

Mom sighs and leans her hands across the table, placing them on top of my own. There is sadness in her eyes as she looks at me, sadness and regret.

"Caroli disease," she says. "That's the name. Very rare and very deadly, they said. It came on suddenly—some kind of esophageal rupture, something with his bile ducts." I shudder; no wonder she tries to avoid thinking about it. Her voice trails off as her eyes water. I can feel her hands tremble on top of mine. "It was awful, Darren. You can tell your doctor that. But you were tested when you were born. You were a perfectly healthy baby."

I stand up, feeling woozy at first, then lean over and kiss the top of her head. She smells like stale beer and cigarette smoke. A wave of guilt and compassion crashes over me, and I suddenly want to do everything I can for her—make early retirement possible, buy her a house in the country, marry and settle down and provide her with grandkids.

"I wouldn't let anything happen to you," she whispers. "You know that." But the last part sounds like a question, voiced in desperation, as if she's trying to convince herself.

"I know. Good night."

I stumble into my bedroom, flopping on top of the bedsheets with damp clothes covering my body. My stomach quivers— I've grown almost used to it by now, and in any case the storm currently raging in my mind overshadows the bodily distress. Despite the nine or so hours I've already slept, I soon crash into unconsciousness. My last thought before lucidity leaves me has to do with my father, strapped to a hospital bed, looking pale and sweaty and monstrous—the man I've only seen in photographs, whose features I can't recall unless his image is before me. How scared he must have been to have everything go wrong so suddenly. How much he must have hated his own body.

Wednesday

I do call in sick to work the next day, telling my boss Charlie that I'm dealing with a stomach virus that can't be tamed. I sound grim and nauseous on the phone, and it's not an act: despite the many hours of sleep the previous night, I wake feeling dizzy and lethargic, and that ever-present throb in my gut is more persistent. Cautiously, as I stand in front of the bathroom mirror and lift my sweaty T-shirt, I prod at my stomach and feel something, I'm sure of it, hard beneath the skin. It's grown since the previous day, this inexplicable mass, and I can swear I see it twitch after I poke at it, a fetus kicking in the womb.

I call Dr. Carstens, and after holding for nearly ten minutes I speak to her directly. I tell her what my mother has relayed: my father died from Caroli disease, which set on suddenly in his mid twenties and could not be treated. I was tested as a newborn and the results were negative. She offers a puzzled grunt on the other end of the line.

"Caroli disease?"

"Yeah, that's what she said."

"That's typically treatable. It shouldn't have killed your father as quickly as it did. What's weirder," she continues, "is that Bryan Trevor's medical records cut off in January of '91. I was able to locate them, but a physical is the last information the

Maryland hospitals have."

"He joined the army around then. Could that be why?"

There's a long pause, weighted with uncertainty. I can hear a muffled voice through the phone.

"Maybe. Do you know where he was treated before he died?"

"Yeah, the Baltimore VA."

"Well, it's possible the army classified those records. But I don't know why if it was Caroli disease." There's a pause, then an exasperated huff. "I'm sorry, Darren. This is turning out to be a bit of a mystery."

She promises to do more digging and call the VA records office, though I can tell by her tone of voice that she's not optimistic. In the meantime, she says, continue with the meds and get plenty of rest. When I come back next week, she adds, we'll run more tests; again, I think to myself that next week is a distant future I might never experience.

As always, Mom left around seven this morning, an hour before I crawled out of bed and struggled to kickstart my body into motion. She left a brief but loving note, telling me to call if I need anything and promising to be home early. She must feel terrible about last night, I assume, terrible and guilty and helpless; I almost call her and leave a heartfelt voicemail, but what would I say?

If I were smart, I would take my medicine and try to rest my weary body. But there's no way I'll confine myself to a bed or a couch today. So, after washing down two more pills and gingerly swallowing a dry English muffin, I open a laptop on the kitchen table and search for Caroli disease. If this was in fact the beast that took my father away, it's not what afflicts me; the facts don't fit. Dilatation of the bile ducts, sometimes accompanied by polycystic kidney disease or liver failure. Yellowing in the skin or abscesses in the liver. I don't exhibit any of these symptoms. And, as Dr. Carstens said, it can usually be treated by surgery or radiation therapy—so why did it steal my father away in a matter of weeks, supposedly?

More doubt, more suspicion.

Our house has a dank, narrow basement, the floors made of stone, the walls oozing a fetid liquid no matter the season. There is a series of shelves against one wall, buckling under the weight of large file boxes that I've been told never to disturb. But of course I have; any child without a father will set out to investigate independently, trying to solve the mystery of the man who's absent.

Many of the files are mundane: insurance information, birth certificates, mortgage paperwork, the detritus left by a life. Another box is filled with old Polaroids of my father, a muscular guy, broad-shouldered, the antithesis of myself; he always seems to be smiling, pronounced dimples, a sparkle in his deep black eyes. Here he's wearing a tuxedo and corsage, leaning against a white limousine, apparently on prom night; here he's grinning and sweating in a football uniform, helmet clutched in his hand. In another he's painting the walls of an empty room, white coveralls and black skin marked with bright blue paint, casting a loving look at the person behind the camera, who I assume to be my mother. In another he has an arm around her shoulders— they're sitting on a dock, feet dangling in the water, beaming up at the unknown photographer as though they're caught off guard. She looks so young, the sun glinting off her green eyes, wearing a two-piece swimsuit, exuding a joy I've only seen in her a few times during my life. He has the grim benefit of always looking young, mummified in his early twenties thanks to these random snapshots, which took on a profound sadness when the person they signify vanished from the world.

The box I'm really looking for, though, is the one stuffed toward the back. It nearly tumbles from my arms as I heave it off the top shelf. It's entirely black, unmarked, and covered with a grimy layer of dust. I've rifled through it before, especially in my middle school years, but it made little sense to me then, and it provoked bursts of outrage from my mother whenever she found me digging through it surreptitiously.

Most of Bryan Trevor's military records are dry and tedious, revealing information that's hardly earth-shattering. At the front is an Enlisted Record & Report of Separation: Bryan Michael Trevor, born November 19, 1972, in Sykesville, MD. Army PFC, 1st Battalion, 18th Infantry Regiment. Date of Entry Into Active Service, December 2, 1990—he was nearly as young as they would allow. He's listed as "Rifleman" and noted for "good conduct" in the Basra theater of Operation Desert Storm. In addition to his immunizations and "returning civilian number" (a piece of data that strikes me as a little too Orwellian), the report lists his Date of Separation with Honorable Discharge as February 11, 1993. This strikes me as odd, considering American troops were pulled out of the Persian Gulf in March of '91—begging the question of what required his prolonged service for nearly two more years.

Next is a Record of Assignments, detailing my father's movements and activities from December 1990 through the first months of '93. The assignment listed for the beginning of that stretch is the 1st Battalion, 18th Infantry Regiment; the theater of war stretches from Rafha, Saudi Arabia, through southeastern Iraq, to Basra and Amarah. But starting in April 1991, thick, heavy swaths of black ink strike through the records, redacting whatever my father did from the official end of the war through February '93. I place the flimsy paper, weighted down with markings, face-down in the file, wondering what my country's military doesn't want me to see.

The next document is even more smothered with ink, as nearly the entire bottom half of the paper is inscribed with neat, draconian lines. It's a letter from a lieutenant colonel named Timothy Stocker; the insignia at the top comes from Fort Riley, Kansas, a red-white-blue coat of arms placed ostentatiously in the corner. Dated January 1993, it starts by commending Bryan Trevor's military service with the 1/18, a battalion at that time commandeered by LTC Stocker. This much I'm able to glean from the unmarked opening paragraph.

After which the entire document is a maze of black lines, a few words standing exposed. Bryan is thanked for volunteering for *something*, the name and details obscured. The final paragraph alludes to the results of the unnamed project, but the data displayed on a table underneath is similarly obliterated. Of course, I think now, it was stupid of me to expect answers from this pile of paperwork; the Powers That Be made sure all sensitive information was scrubbed away before the papers were released to the public.

It's at this point that I double over in pain, hand reaching for my gut as I sit cross-legged on concrete. What a pathetic image I must be, minuscule beneath the bright, bare bulb hanging from the ceiling. Something squirms inside, a knot that tightens and expands from my intestines to stomach to esophagus. At least my physical and emotional pain appear to be working in tandem.

A few minutes later I struggle to my feet, legs shaky, hands pushing against the floor to stand. I drag myself up the wooden stairs, the railing barely supporting my weight. Make it to the kitchen, shuffle across the floor, collapse in a chair at the table.

What has been redacted from my father's life? And has it been reborn somewhere deep inside me? In order to chase it down, I think at last, I have to go back to the end for my father—back to his death. The Baltimore VA Medical Center is a thirty-minute bus ride downtown. As long as my body cooperates that long, this seems like the logical next step.

I throw on another T-shirt (this one less drenched in sweat) and a pair of long black shorts, then step outside. It's hot again today—it feels like every day outduels the last in scorching humidity. The sun beats down as I trudge to Frederick and Wickham, then pick up the purple CityLink bus. It rumbles through historic Irvington and Union Square, past the stately 19th century house of H.L. Mencken. Finally downtown approaches, and the bus pulls up outside the long, glass-and-concrete building that is the Baltimore VA Medical Center. There's a protest this afternoon, as there has been several times a week for about half a year; streets are blocked off as people march in righteous indignation. Many carry papier-mâché effigies of pigs wearing police gear and wave signs reading "KLUELESS KILLER KOPS" and "THE WHOLE DAMN SYSTEM IS GUILTY AS HELL." Others, a small but ferocious congregation, raise thin-blue-line flags and wear gas masks and combat boots. The animosity has intensified this year as the presidential election looms. Whoever is voted in this fall, there will be hell to pay on the streets and in our cities. The collapse of the American empire has to begin somehow.

The bus rounds the corner to avoid protesters, inching around cones and stanchions, passengers squinting out the windows with looks of rage or solidarity.

The lobby of the VA hospital looks immaculate on the surface, tile floors recently waxed, speckled walls gleaming in the sun—it all looks a little too well-polished. An unshaven man with a Vietnam Vet hat slouches in a chair near the corner, chin resting on his hand, eyes dull and empty as he stares ahead. Down two rows, a woman with her legs amputated at the knees sits in a wheelchair, fidgeting nervously; a man sits next to her, flipping through *Outdoor Life* magazine. A few seats away, a Black woman in a well-tailored, pearl-colored suit sits with her right leg crossed over her knee, a book spread open on her lap. I can't help but wonder about them, conjecturing what it is they're going through while realizing how presumptuous it is to do so. I've heard stories about the VA, censorious news reports and calls for reform. I know that some veterans wait fourteen months or more for an urgent appointment, or they're not deemed enough of a "risk" to receive the medications that can make the pain and suicidal impulses go away. I know some veterans show up for appointments a year in the making, venturing long distances, only to be told that their appointment's been canceled last-minute and they have to wait another year for the next one. I know there is a tendency to peddle pharmaceuticals instead of providing holistic medicine and psychiatric care. But I don't know what it's like to need health care from this hospital, and I don't know how it feels to return from military duty and face apathy from so many who think they understand.

The admittance desk is my destination, a wide, narrow window beckoning ahead of me. Soft, yellow light pours from it. A few employees in white coats idle there in rolling chairs, one of them holding a quiet, seething conversation on the phone. Her coworker, a brown-haired woman with kind blue eyes, looks up as I approach.

"Hi, can I help you?" She has a low-pitched voice and a Southern drawl. Her nametag reads Kathy.

"Hi. Yeah, I'm looking for some information about my dad. He was admitted here a long time ago."

"Mmkay. What's his name?"

"Bryan Trevor." Kathy pecks at her keyboard. There is a long silence, filled with the phlegmy coughing of someone in the lobby. "I think he was admitted in, uh . . . must've been November of '98."

She arches her eyebrows and nods. "I see. Well I gotta tell ya, our records from back then ain't exactly *pristine*. We tried to digitize 'em all but I don't think it's ever gonna happen."

I waver there, growing exhausted. There's a new, encroaching pain, not sharp and stabbing but slow and insidious.

"I'll see what I can find, though. Bryan Trevor, you said?"

I nod. "T-r-e-v-o-r."

"Sit tight," she says, springing from her chair and moving through a doorway into a rear office.

She's gone for a while—ten minutes, though it seems much longer. In her absence, I roam the sun-drenched lobby. There's a folding table set up against the far wall, attended by a gaunt and wiry man with large glasses and a shiny bald head. A banner reading W.H.V., "Welcome Home Veterans," hangs from the table. The cursive letters are blue, the insignia red, the background white, an obligatory color scheme. The table is littered with resources for veterans: pamphlets detailing community events and support groups, plastic cases to organize pills by date and dosage, books written by war heroes and psychologists, daily planners and journals with images of rustic American frontiers.

"Can I help you find something?" The man's voice is nasally

but soothing. He squints from behind his oversized lenses.

"No thanks." A brochure about a horse farm in southern Maryland catches my eye; the cover has a picture of a man with a long gray beard stroking a handsome thoroughbred, love and trust in both their eyes.

"Looking for a friend or relative?" the man asks. I realize then I don't look like a typical war veteran.

I decide to evade the truth. "My dad."

"Whatever he needs, we can help."

I nod, touched by his sincerity. Before I can respond, Kathy at the welcome desk calls me back with a polite and adamant, "Sir?"

As I approach the window, she tells me the words I've been dreading.

"I'm sorry, Mr. Trevor, those records are classified."

"Classified."

She clicks her tongue. "Afraid even next of kin don't have access."

"Okay," I say with a long sigh, feeling too weak to protest. Before turning away, I ask another question. "Um . . . did it say who his doctor was?"

"Sure, that was Dr. Sharp. Henry Sharp."

"Okay, I'll see if I can find him. Thanks."

"Oh, I can call him down for you, see if he's available."

I pause mid-pivot, not sure if I heard correctly. "He's still here?"

"Oh yeah," she chirps in response, "our longest tenured physician. Must have been a rookie when he saw your dad."

I stand there in silence, mouth hanging open; is it possible I've had a stroke of good luck? My stomach contorts in response, *there's no good luck for you, you sorry son of a bitch,* and I'm forced to reach my hand out to support myself against the ledge of the window. Oblivious, Kathy picks up a white phone and punches a few numbers, then speaks with someone on the other end.

I hunch in a small plastic seat as I wait, reading *The Metamorphosis* again. *I cannot make anyone understand what is happening inside me. I cannot even explain it to myself.* Kafka knew a few things. Can I make you understand the loneliness I'm feeling, the sense of cosmic absurdity that's gathered in force these last few days? Can I explain to myself how growing up fatherless set me adrift, even as I tried to convince myself that it had no impact whatsoever? Somewhere in the sweltering morass of my brain, the most difficult thought processes take place—the rumbling machinations through which I try to comprehend my state of being. It's here that I start to feel old and defeated at not-quite-twenty-five, my father's mortality making me all too aware of my expiration date.

After twenty more minutes of gloomy contemplation, Dr. Sharp finally appears, a thin Black man with a kindly face and short, gray hair. I'm the only guest lingering in the lobby at this point. He strides up to me and shoots out his hand. I shake it slowly, palm damp with sweat, as I rise to my feet. I see him look at me askew, concern in his eyes.

"Hi, sorry to make you wait. You're . . ."

"Darren."

"Darren. I'm Dr. Sharp. Kathy told me you had some questions about your dad."

I nod, dizzy from the effort.

"What's his name?"

"Bryan Trevor. He was—"

"Bryan Trevor, you said?"

I nod again.

"Must've been . . . what, '98?"

"Yeah. He died in November that year."

"I remember, yeah. How could I forget?"

"So, there was something weird about it?" I ask.

Dr. Sharp opens his mouth to answer; looks at the floor, then the ceiling, the windows; and lets out a brief, emphatic sigh. "Why don't you come up to my office?"

I do; the walk and the elevator ride are mostly silent, footsteps clacking and machinery humming. He mentions the steamy weather, a conversation that goes nowhere; and he asks if I'm feeling okay, a question I evade with a shrug. "Been feeling kinda off, I guess."

We reach his office on the third floor, a claustrophobic room with buzzing white lights, a narrow hospital bed, and a plastic desk littered with pictures of his radiant family. He sits on a wheeled chair and spins until he's facing me, placing his hands on his lap, fingers interlocked. I heave myself onto the hospital bed with a painful lurch, feeling my bowels jostle inside me. I glance at my reflection in a mirror on the wall and find the beady, hollow eyes of an unknown creature staring back.

"So. Bryan Trevor."

I look back at Dr. Sharp. "You remember him?" I ask again.

"He's not the sort of thing you forget. I had only started my residency here two months earlier. At that time, in '98, you had a lot of vets coming in with Gulf War syndrome. The causes were unknown, but the symptoms were familiar: headaches, memory loss, fatigue, muscle pain. A lot of them started to develop, over the next couple years, malignant tumors. But your dad was something else. What do you know about his death?"

"Not much. Just yesterday, my mom told me he died of Caroli

disease. That's all I know."

Dr. Sharp frowns and shakes his head. "It wasn't that. Abdominal pain is about the *only* symptom that corresponds. That must've been a smokescreen, and not a very good one."

"What do you mean?"

He pauses then, looking just past me, toward the closed door. Then he speaks, quietly, clearly.

"Your father came in with severe stomach pain, I remember that. It started about a week before he died. It was strange—he had returned from the Middle East several years earlier, isn't that right?"

I nod woozily. "Yeah, he came home in February of '93. I looked at his records earlier today. I thought that was weird; most of the ground troops pulled out in early '91."

"Right. So he had been home a little more than five years and, as he told me during his first visit, his health was relatively good. Especially in comparison to some other veterans. Do you mind if I ask—when were you born?"

"June 14th of '99. He died just after my mom got pregnant."

Dr. Sharp nods profoundly, without pity. I'm thankful that he doesn't offer any empty apologies. "He was healthy, apparently, when you were conceived. If it was Caroli disease, there would have been symptoms for years beforehand, and it should have been easily treatable."

"Okay." I struggle to keep my confusion at bay; I want to scream obscenities to disturb the silence. "What happened then?"

"He got worse, very quickly. Extreme discomfort, vomiting blood, unable to digest anything. Fatigue, headaches, dizziness. There . . . seemed to be some kind of tissue growing in his stomach. And in the last couple days, he said, it behaved erratically."

I stare at the doctor. My brain is unable to form words.

"We brought him into surgery. Strapped him down. He was in a lot of pain. We tried to sedate him, but there wasn't time. He was saying a lot of things that didn't make sense. 'This is the next stage,' or something like that. I asked him what it was. Something about Operation Echidna. 'Echidna worked,' I think he said."

He swallows hard. So do I.

"What then?"

"I was ready to operate without anesthesia. Your mother was outside the O.R. She had trouble controlling herself, understandably. We had a few guards restraining her. I remember the scalpel broke the dermis, and something responded inside of him."

"Responded?"

"Something in the GI tract. Like a defense mechanism. Then there was a commotion outside. Some military commander came in, along with his men, all armed, assault rifles, everything. He brought in two of his own doctors in armored HAZMATs. Ordered us to leave immediately."

"You're fucking kidding me."

The doctor shakes his head. He bristles at the memory. "Confidential military matter, he said. I was furious. There was no way I was going to leave that O.R., not after what I saw. But . . . I was young. A man's career can be ruined. And a private pointing an AK at you while you're standing in your scrubs can be pretty convincing."

"So they took over."

Dr. Sharp shrugs, lifting his hands. "I guess so. Maybe they tried to operate. Maybe not. In any case, after what I saw, survival didn't seem like a possibility."

"You never saw him again." I mean it as a question but it comes out declamatory.

The doctor shakes his head, confirming my assumption. "Afterward—when the nurses and I had cleaned up, we were all in sort of a daze—your mother asked me what happened. I didn't know what to say."

There's another long silence in the room. The silence of a crime scene, heavy with violence and disgust. I'm surprised by Dr. Sharp's animus, even after all these years.

"So what do you think it was?"

Dr. Sharp stands, smoothing out his white coat, and steps toward me. "Anything I say would be conjecture. And it was made clear to me that I'm not to speak to anyone about this—a threat I remember well. But something was done to your father, I have no doubt about that."

I stand then too, with great difficulty, twisting my body, feeling pain and nausea resurface.

"I'm grateful, but . . . why are you telling me this? If you were threatened to stay silent."

He sighs and a somber look comes over him, bright eyes suddenly weighed down by resignation. "You're his son, after all, and it was a generation ago. But that's just it. I'm getting old and I keep seeing the same things over and over. So the short answer is, I'm getting sick of it. I'm a Band-Aid on an oil spill."

We look at each other. I smile meekly, a forced gesture, but sincere.

"You sure you're okay?" He grimaces at me again, more urgent this time.

"Yeah. Well, no. Um, there's no chance what happened to him will . . . happen to me, is there?"

Dr. Sharp tries to look nonchalant, but I can tell there is gravity in his expression. When he speaks, it sounds like he's trying to convince himself. "I don't see how it could. You were tested as an infant, right?"

"Yeah."

"Yeah. If you want, though, we can run some tests . . ."

"No, I saw a doctor yesterday. I'm taking some meds." It's that, and also the fact that I'm tired as hell; I struggle to keep my eyes open, my muscles and joints ache, I see patches of blackness and a blurry fog before my eyes. A series of tests and more time spent at the hospital sound like prolonged torture. At the same time, though, I begin to feel a strange, buzzing energy, an uncanny communion with everything around me, as if the world now appears to me in a new and heightened way. I feel at once electric and enervated. All I can do is thank Dr. Sharp and lurch out the door, one step after another. He hands me his card before I leave and offers to help however he can—his words carry countless emotions, alarm and anger and apology. Seconds later, in the hallway, I struggle to remember everything he's told me. It takes all my effort to remain focused as I plummet to the ground floor in the elevator and stumble through the lobby out to the street with an abominable fury inside my gut.

Thursday

As it was throughout my youth, the library becomes my refuge: a way to escape the confines of my city, a shelter from the surrounding storm. I remember the route to the Enoch Pratt Library well: a few blocks west to Athol Avenue, then about a mile north to Edmondson. I scuttle past the New Cathedral Cemetery on the way, its gravestones a stark reminder of the fate I know awaits me.

It's a good thing the jaunt is brief; my body can't handle any more. I barely slept throughout the night, my organs a jangle of aches and terrors. I tossed, turned, flailed from one side of the bed to the other, throttled against my will; I feel there's some merciless being inside me, jerking my strings like a marionette.

So this is what it feels like to have your body mutiny, to doubt every second that the basic acts of living—respiration, heartbeat, circulation, brainwaves—are still under your control. My grandpa on my mother's side, Harris, died of pancreatic cancer when I was only four, and since I barely knew him, the fact of his death never registered to me, the words didn't signify anything. But now, maybe, I have a sense of what Harris went through: the mounting fear as his body broke down, those basic elements of life taken for granted so many years cruelly snatched away. Restless nights as you lie in bed, not knowing if you'll wake up again.

Was it the same for my father? Did Bryan Trevor feel trapped inside his failing body at only twenty-four years old? I shuffle down the sidewalk, dragging one foot after the other, my red T-shirt heavy with sweat. From under the fabric, I think I see a protuberance poke at the inside of my gut, straining against flesh to achieve its liberation.

And yet, that same preternatural energy remains, a oneness with the world and the living things around me. The heat is oppressive, but comfortably so—as if this is the habitat in which I belong. I pass an assemblage of people on the sidewalks, a tired single mother waiting for the bus, a weary old man who wants only the solace of death, a desperate young man who's dangerously close to robbing somebody at gunpoint, and I feel they tell me their entire life story through a momentary glance.

I stumble into the Enoch Pratt Library, knowing how awful I look. I attract a few questioning stares, but no one says anything. This is why I love libraries: a hideous creature with scaly skin and daggers for hands could slither through the front door and everyone would give it a respectful distance. I drag myself to one of the computers and type out a few keyword searches, holding my arm against my stomach as if trying to keep its contents inside.

I don't know exactly what I'm searching for, aside from the vague conspiracy theories that have popped up in my battered mind. *Gulf War, military experiments, hereditary symptoms*—one subject leads to another, a rabbit hole of alarming facts.

Before long I have a stack of books amassed on a long table, carried there in my cradled arms as I shuffle woozily over thin carpet. I begin with the basics of the Gulf War, most of which I know already: coalition forces entered Kuwait and then Iraq, resulting in a ceasefire after barely more than five weeks of combat. But the fallout would last much longer for those on both sides of the conflict. Over a thousand Kuwaiti and three thousand Iraqi civilians were killed, including four hundred in an Amiriyah bunker bombed by American stealth planes. After the war, tens of thousands more civilians died from political chaos and the destruction of basic infrastructure. (The numbers are hard to quantify, reads one of my sources, because the US government refused to release its own study of the public health crisis that ensued.)

Upon ceasefire and the return of American soldiers, the impacts of Gulf War syndrome became apparent over time. Veterans were more likely to suffer from multiple sclerosis and brain cancer, though the links to the war were never definitively proven. More prevalent were supposedly minor symptoms like constant pain, nausea, fatigue—not quite treatable and more destructive because of it. The causes were debated hotly: pesticide use in the Middle East, sarin gas, airborne toxins spread by the burning of oil wells. But the answer may never be proved exactly, and my beleaguered mind finds this appropriate—a deadly origin more symbolic than literal.

It's all sobering information, but not exactly what I'm looking for. What did my father encounter during his extended tour of duty to cut short his life so ruthlessly? The little parasite in my gut convulses at this thought, tapping at the inside of my abdominal walls. I shudder and groan, causing a few wary glances to look my way. I press my open palm against the fabric of my shirt and feel something on the other side, undeniable this time, making violent zigzags across my nerve endings.

I force myself to focus and flip through a few more books, allowing my eyes to wander. I brush up on the sinister experiments our military has conducted upon its own people. Mustard gas experiments on American soldiers in Panama, forced to venture into wooden chambers and doused with chemicals that burned through their skin. Hospital patients fed or injected with polonium and plutonium, including mentally handicapped children, then studied to chart their inevitable decay. Lightbulbs filled with *bacillus globigii* thrown onto New York subway tracks to see what would happen when the bacteria spread throughout the city. A diabolical surgeon who experimented on the inmates of San Quentin Prison, implanting the testicles of rams, goats, and boars into living prisoners. Project Bluebird, whereby the military tested "enhanced interrogation" techniques on soldiers, using hypnosis, morphine, LSD, mescaline, a smorgasbord of psychotropics to extract information from unwilling subjects. MK-ULTRA, the Tuskegee experiments, Operation Top Hat . . . the list goes on. By the time I'm done reading about them, my conspiracy theories don't seem so farfetched.

In my hasty research, conducted through a haze of pain and fatigue, I also discover Fort Detrick, which is located not sixty miles away in Frederick, Maryland. It just so happens that Fort Detrick has housed America's biological weapons program since 1943. Samples of ebola and smallpox are stored there; there's even a building known as Anthrax Tower, which was used to produce some five thousand bombs containing anthrax spores during World War II. When enlisted soldiers stopped volunteering for the experiments at Fort Detrick (which were collectively known as Operation Whitecoat), the army began recruiting conscientious objectors to be the victims of biological tests without their knowledge.

More relevant to my immediate predicament are the number

of tests involving insects for the purpose of biological warfare. German and Japanese scientists looking to escape persecution after World War II found refuge in Fort Detrick, where they and their American brethren dropped infected fleas, ticks, ants, lice, and mosquitoes upon unwitting people in the United States—or injected them directly into the bloodstreams of unlucky hospital patients.

The motherfucker in my stomach heaves against my innards, and I swear I feel something tear within my sweating, weakened body.

I discover something else about Fort Detrick: a list of military personnel at the base counts Colonel Timothy Stocker as its commanding officer. I wonder for a moment where I've seen that name, until it occurs to me: Bryan Trevor's commanding officer during his extended stay in Iraq and Saudi Arabia. The redacted files in the basement of my home come back to me: Colonel Stocker is the man who officially thanked my dad for volunteering for *something* in the wake of the war.

I've exhausted the stack of references on my library table, having learned nothing about covert military experiments upon Gulf War soldiers from the spring of 1991 through the winter of '93. I shouldn't be surprised, I think with a frown: the military wouldn't allow information of that sort to find its way into public libraries.

As my weary eyes drift around the room, something catches my eye: a rack of magazines tucked into the corner. Most of them are mainstream magazines with glitzy covers meant to catch the reader's eye. But, like most libraries, this one has a healthy rebellious streak, and there are a few local agitprop publications tucked alongside the *Times* and *Fortunes*. I rise to my feet with a dizzy tremor and limp to the corner of the room. The title of one magazine leaps out at me, in bold yellow font against a red background: *The Equator.* On the inside front cover, the magazine proudly mentions its lineage to a Black newspaper founded by Weldy Walker in the nineteenth century. There are news articles, op ed pieces, arts reviews, and muckraking essays purporting to speak to social justice in the Baltimore area. One article mentions a backroom deal between the local police union and a shady politician whose donations somehow arranged for the police to buy a new and indestructible armored tank. Another proposes that a new virus called the Vigo strain was intentionally added to Charlottesville's water supply to see how it would affect the public. They seem like wild conjecture but also, as I flip through the magazine and lean lifelessly against the wall, entirely plausible. I turn to the masthead, hoping but not expecting to find anything like reliable contact info; but lo and behold, there's a shipping address tucked into the lower left corner of the page. It's located in Dundalk, an expanse southeast of the city littered with abandoned factories and shuttered homes. It's a gamble, but I tell myself that if anyone in Baltimore would have insight into covert military experiments, it would be the publishers of this magazine.

Before I can develop any plan of action, the pain in my gut becomes too intense to bear. I throw the magazine onto the carpet and lurch toward the bathroom, leaning on tables and bookshelves for support. This time, a librarian stands behind the front desk and moves in my direction, offering an urgent, "Sir!"

I burst into the bathroom just in time, collapsing to my knees, lifting the toilet seat, and spraying a geyser of bright red vomit into the spotless porcelain. It's a pain I've never known before, every speck of my being convulsed from the waist up. My bodily distress is no longer a secondary concern, held at bay as my mind does cartwheels. By this point, the pain has become paramount.

At this moment, my phone rings, buzzing in my pocket. With my head leaning on my forearm, trails of redness dripping, I pull out the device. Shannon is calling. I start to place the phone back in my pocket; the last thing I want to do is maintain appearances when I feel like literal death. But the truth occurs to me. I need help. I have few friends in my life to call on during times like this—a product of my self-imposed hermetism. And in these lowest depths, I know I need the company of another to feel like a human once again.

I answer the call and mutter into plastic.

"Hello?"

The pause on the other end is heavy with concern.

"Darren?"

"Yeah."

"Are you okay?"

I swallow. "Not really."

"You don't sound like it."

"Yeah. I'm currently . . ." I fortify myself for the impending conversation. "I'm on the floor of the bathroom in the Enoch Pratt Library on Edmondson. I just threw up a pint of blood in the toilet."

"Jesus." There's a knock at the bathroom door and an urgent voice saying, *Everything okay in there?* "I was worried when you weren't at work. Now I'm . . . even more worried."

For days I've shut true terror out of mind, telling myself that stoic resolve is the honorable thing to do. (If Bryan Trevor were alive, would he tell me the same thing? It's a rare moment in which I fantasize about the moral guidance a father might provide.) But now, tears stream down my face. I'm scared. I know this thing inside me is not right, not normal. Mortality becomes a tangible presence.

"I think I . . . I'm sorry to ask this. I need help."

"Of course." She says it without a moment's hesitation. It occurs to me that she deserves better, she shouldn't waste her time on a pitiable case like me. But I say:

"Can you pick me up? There's somewhere I need to go."

"Yeah. You mean the hospital?"

I say nothing. There's no way I can explain over the phone.

"Darren," she says. "You better fucking say the hospital."

"I'll explain when you get here," I mutter.

* * *

Thirty minutes later, I'm curled up in the fetal position in Shannon's red Honda, watching the scenery pass by. The intervening time was spent cleaning up the spatter of viscera in the bathroom and assuring the librarians that help was on the way. The impostor in my stomach (whom I've started calling Gregor in honor of Franz K.) has settled down somewhat. But I still know he's there, like a disruptive neighbor who could start banging on the walls at any moment.

"Tell me again why we're not going to the hospital."

Shannon drives with her hands at ten and two, clutching the steering wheel so hard I can see her knuckles whiten. Through the windows, I see yet another protest that has fallen into altercation: a peaceful march has been disrupted by fascist demonstrators, who proudly wear flak vests, gas masks, and combat boots. As we speed past, someone swings a two-by-four upward, hitting a middle-aged woman square in her jaw. These spectacles of violence are happening more often. Nearly every day, there's a clash of people warring on the streets; the breaking point is no longer hypothetical, but clear and present.

Shannon leans forward into my line of sight, snapping me back to my own grim reality. There's something like anger in her expression—anger at someone who cares little for self-preservation.

It takes me a while to answer. "I think the place we're going will have more answers than a doctor could give me."

"Right," she says irritably. "What would a doctor know? Some wild goose chase is a way better idea."

"This thing inside of me," I mutter through clenched teeth, "it's not normal. I know that, Shannon, with total certainty. I need to go somewhere else for answers."

"You know what you sound like?" She tries to peer directly at me and keep her eyes on the road at the same time. "Some paranoid conspiracy theorist who wants to feel better about himself by inventing wild explanations. Did it occur to you that you have a disease a doctor could treat?"

"It occurred to me a couple days ago," I say, the words coming from the miasma in my gut. "I'm past that point now."

"Ah. Enlightened, huh?"

"Listen." I twist toward her, my body a jangle of raw nerves. I feel something push back inside of me. "I owe you big time. I know that. I'm sorry. I just want to see if I can find out anything here. Then afterwards, I'll go to the hospital. You don't even have to drive me—I'll find a way."

She sighs heavily. "I don't *mind* driving you, Darren. It's not that. I just . . . don't think you're doing the right thing. There's an easier way to solve this."

I shake my head. "My dad couldn't solve it."

She grows silent at this cryptic response. We say almost nothing as she drives another twenty minutes to the wasteland of Dundalk southeast of the city.

The address of *The Equator* is a sprawling brick building that seems void of life: shutters over the windows, weeds breaking through concrete, stains on the edifice from unknown sources. There's graffiti on the walls, too. The more recent lettering, in bold spray paint, is especially violent: DEATH TO PROUD BOYS and KEEP AMERIKKKA WHITE battling on the brick surface, letters like corpses. There's a marquee on the front lawn with no letters on it and sports equipment in the rear—some basketball courts, a soccer field. I remember, now, hearing about a community college that folded in the late teens, but no one could (or wanted to) buy the property. And so a massive building with significant resources lay dormant—a fate similar to the countless other buildings in the city that loom as shells of their former selves.

"This is it?" Shannon asks as she inches into the parking lot, more than a trace of skepticism in her voice.

"I hope so."

Her tires crunch over gravel and urban flora as she pulls up close to a front entryway. She cuts the ignition and springs from the car. I try, but I can no longer twist my body the way it needs to go. She walks to the passenger side and helps me out, her hand lightly grasping my frail, sweaty wrist. I lean against the car as I stand. Something happens I don't expect: Shannon leans in close, wrapping her arms around my body, and puts her lips against my ear. I can feel her eyelids flutter against my cheek.

"Please. There's nothing here."

"I need to know what's happening to me."

She pulls away, tears in her eyes. Opens her mouth to say something. Then looks at the ground and shakes her head.

"Let's get this over with then."

The front doors are chained and reinforced with a heavy padlock, but there are faint noises inside, we hear as we approach: heated conversation, intermittent bangs and clangs, the whir of chugging machinery. Shannon and I skirt the outside of the building, looking for an entryway. In the rear, we find a pair of wide doors by a dumpster, one of which is propped open with an orange traffic cone.

We creep inside, permitting a blast of sunlight into the building. It looks like a sleepy college campus: polished floors, buzzing lights, flyers for various student groups that probably haven't met for a decade. There's a mellow hum coming from upstairs and a large staircase beckoning to the right. As we ascend it, we notice the walls are lined with the Palestinian flag, portraits of Malcolm X and Assata Shakur, Black Lives Matter banners, scrawled slogans from *The Wretched of the Earth:* "a government gets the people it deserves and sooner or later a people gets the government it deserves."

There's more activity on the second floor: echoes down the hallways, shadows moving in the distance, muffled conversations in nearby rooms.

Shannon leans closer and whispers in my ear. "So what is this place? Some militant journal?"

"As far as I know." I turn in her direction and she recoils against her will—a sign of how revolting I look. "Let's find out."

We sidle down the hallway, looking for traces of life. In one room, we peek around the corner of the doorway and find about a dozen people seated in a circle of chairs. They appear to be in the middle of an ardent debate.

". . . peaceful protests aren't the thing anymore. Their futility has been proven. A ruling class that only understands violence can only be swayed by violence."

Another voice, female, counters in response: "We can't condone taking innocent lives. That makes us just as bad as our oppressors."

"*Innocent* lives, yeah," says another woman. In fact, it appears the whole congregation is female, most of them wearing heavy black boots and military camo. "But the guilty deserve their own punishment. And not only lives. Buildings, police stations, banks, prisons—burn 'em all down."

There's chatter of agreement among the small crowd. "Brick and plaster. Fuck it. Destroy it. Economic impact is all they're gonna recognize."

"Empty fireworks," says another voice, rising above the crowd. "They'll put up barb wire and use force against us, and then people will say that they're justified. The only real change comes from legislation."

"What the fuck do laws matter?" asks a furious voice. "You expect an unjust system to care about us?"

The furor continues as Shannon and I move away, further down the hall. My depression deepens, a futility that extends to bodies other than my own.

A few rooms down, we hear a machine panting loudly and encounter a real live printing press, spitting out copies of a new publication. Only ten feet in front us, we spot hundreds of copies of *The Equator* reproduced on high-quality paper, Toni Bond on the cover accompanied by her words: "We all have a human right to make decisions about our bodies."

I feel a pressure at the back of my head before I can respond.

It's small, metallic, forceful, extended as a threat. I know it's a gun barrel before I turn around. From the gasp next to me, I know there's a similar object pressed against the back of Shannon's head.

"You have ten seconds to explain why you're here."

There's a shuffling of feet and the holding of breath. Even the tall, gaunt woman operating the printing press shuts it down immediately, stepping toward the door and gawking at us.

Words can't come to me for several seconds, and I wonder if this is the merciful end. Then I say:

"I'm looking for answers. I think I'm in danger."

"Damn right you are," says a different voice behind us. But the threat of murder seems to have dissipated. "Turn around."

Shannon and I twist our bodies. Everything seems woozy and crooked, not only due to my physical ailments.

Staring us in the face are four women, wearing similar regalia as the militant philosophers in the classroom down the hall. Two of them are Black, one white, another looks like me, skin color ambiguous.

"You're looking for answers in the wrong place," says one of them as she stares me down, her eyes in shadow from the brim of a black beret.

I shake my head. "You're the only ones who can help me."

* * *

Ten minutes later, we're in another empty classroom; the posters on the walls and books lining a few shelves suggest this used to be a biology lab. (*Biology*, my mind thinks, racing faster than my sluggish body; if only human life could be fully explained by biological processes, eat sleep fuck die, no complications in between.) A few others have joined us, three more women sitting in uncomfortable chairs or leaning against the walls, eyeing us warily. Two of them carry AR-15s, weapons that are easy to find in an empire of death.

After nearly a minute of threatening silence, I take the initiative to speak up, a hum of machinery echoing down the still hallway outside.

I tell them about my father, PFC Bryan Trevor, who stayed in Iraq and Saudi Arabia for more than two years after the end of hostilities in '91. I tell them about his mysterious death, his totally senseless diagnosis, the intervention of armed soldiers, his expiration on his twenty-fifth birthday. I tell them about Operation Echidna, the words my father said in the hospital before he died. I tell them about my own worsening health, the lump in my gut and the bloody vomit, the feeling that there's an intruder in my body. I tell them I'm only a day away from my own twenty-fifth birthday. I pause frequently throughout my monologue, catching my breath and nearly passing out from fatigue.

"Why don't you see a doctor?" asks a voice across the room, sitting behind a now-dormant desk.

Shannon slaps her hands against her knees, the first noise she's made since guns were trained on us. "See! The revolution agrees with me."

I shake my head and pause. "I can't really explain it. But I know whatever this is . . . it's not really medical. You know? We understand each other, this thing inside me."

The woman in the black beret snickers across from me, a scornful laugh. She leans back in her plastic folding chair, crossing her legs in front of her. I can't blame her incredulity.

"Seriously," she says. "Why do you think we can help you?"

"You're . . . I mean, I read your paper. *The Equator.* You know about these things, right? The crimes they don't want us to know. You're trying to expose them."

There's another derisive laugh to the left of me, even more violent this time, and it takes me a second to realize that Shannon has uttered it. "You know what you sound like, Darren?" she asks, leaning forward in her chair. Her eyes exude compassion, but the words sound harsh and angry. "Some guy who *can* help himself, he has friends and resources, but he invents reasons—"

The woman in the black beret holds her hand in Shannon's direction. "Hold up."

"—for his bad situation. 'Poor me, the world is against me.' Help yourself!"

A tall, blond woman leaning against a chalkboard smiles wryly. "Your accomplice is skeptical."

Shannon turns toward her and half-rises from her orange plastic chair. "I'm nobody's fucking accomplice." The blond woman shrugs. I can't help but smile. I admire Shannon more with each passing moment, then wonder how many more of them I'll have with her.

"I want you to explain," says the woman in the beret, refusing to look away from me. I get the sense she's the leader, if they have such a thing, of this makeshift cabal. "How do you know this isn't an ulcer? Or stomach cancer? Or some bad fucking gorditas you had last night?"

I smile at the bad joke, then choose my words carefully. I've never even thought them before, but now I'm saying them out loud. "I've never known my dad. He died before I was born. But I feel like I know what happened to him, like it's some part of my genetic code or something. Does that make sense? The doctors couldn't help him."

"But that's because the army stepped in," says the woman in the beret. "They don't know about you. Right? Or they'd be knocking down your door already."

I shrug. "I guess you're right." I swallow. It's painful. "Somehow, I think this is meant to be. Like I was born for this."

Shannon scoffs again. "Delusions of grandeur."

"I want to know more about you," I say to the woman in the beret before anyone can respond. "Your . . . collective. Please."

There's another long pause. In the yard outside, I can hear chanting, a rhythmic, militaristic marching. The woman in the beret rises and moves toward the window. The sun glides across her skin. "What's there to say? Things have gotten worse. My dad was killed by the police. A raid on the building he lived in. They were executing a warrant on somebody else. My mom was beaten on the street because she was wearing a hijab. Nobody helps. You try to find a lawyer, you go to the newspapers, but these things don't bring publicity. There's no value in it for the people who have power. And if there's no value for them, it's not gonna happen." She turns back to me, her movements calm and composed but her eyes fiery. "It's like Assata says. 'Dreams and reality are opposites. Action synthesizes them.' Dreams of freedom, hope, humanity. They confront the powers of reality, which will crush the life out of you and bury you in secret. That's what we're trying to take down."

Another pause, long enough to make me realize the beast in my gut is strangely placid. "Me too. I never wanted that before this week. But now I do."

She shifts the beret atop her head and wanders slowly to the chair across from me, collapsing into it, leaning forward, elbows on her knees.

"Operation Echidna, you said?" I nod, my excitement rising to the surface, though I'm sure my lethargic appearance conceals it. "I've heard of it. One of our hackers broke into a government server a few years ago. I can show you the reports we found. Test results from '95, I think. Commanding officer was Timothy Stocker—that was the name you said, right? The experiments go back a lot further than that, though. Our military's played around with xenotransplantation since the '50s, at least."

"Xenotrans . . ."

"Fusing of human tissue with other biological entities."

"You mean, like putting a sheep's heart in a human body?"

"Yeah, that's the medical reasoning. The kind you hear about on the news. But there's another kind. Splicing the DNA of other creatures into human subjects—predators, microbes, insects, you name it. You know how ants can carry up to five thousand times their own body weight? Imagine if a soldier could do that. Or use echolocation like a bat. Regenerate severed limbs like an iguana."

"The ultimate fighting machine," says another voice from the corner of the room.

"Bullshit," Shannon spits out. "Science fiction."

"It's only fiction 'til it's non-fiction," says the woman in the beret. "And America's known for its suspension of disbelief."

"What are you saying?" I ask. "My dad was a test subject?"

The woman in the beret nods. "Soldiers were offered a substantial pay raise if they stayed on for medical experiments. They weren't told the details, only that they'd receive an injection that would alter their biological makeup, for the better supposedly. Their genome was shifted for the sake of national security—infused with the DNA of *Blattella germanica*."

"*Blattella* what?" I ask.

"German cockroach."

Once again, I swallow roughly. The pain is greater, mixed with a newfound terror. The monster in my gut kicks again, a mocking movement.

"German fucking what?" Shannon asks.

"Cockroach," says the ringleader, missing Shannon's rhetorical point. "It's a species known for its social structure—communicates with other specimens through clicks and sounds, even mental functioning. It's able to withstand extreme heat and cold, not to mention severe injury—dismemberment or being crushed under immense weight."

"You've got to be . . ." Shannon began.

"More to the point, though, they have chemoreceptors that can pick up on airborne toxins, chemicals, that sort of thing. Which is probably why the military was playing around with it. Detect serin gas and biological warfare."

A long silence follows. How do you follow up such information? I should be shocked, but my limited amount of research has prepared me for any kind of barbarism.

Shannon breaks the silence, rising from her chair and racing toward me in three quick steps. A few of the soldiers in the room lift their rifles, then lower them when they've deemed Shannon to be non-threatening.

"Darren, I don't know what the fuck is going on, but this is an even better reason to get your ass to a hospital. They put you under, they cut this thing out of you, end of story."

I shake my head. "Then the story gets buried. That's no ending."

She shakes her head, practically spitting rabid froth, and paces in a circle. "It's a happy ending for you! Because you don't fucking *die*, dumbass."

This provokes another strain of thought in my beleaguered mind. "So why *did* he die? My dad, I mean. The experiment didn't go well, I guess."

The woman across from me shrugs; there seems to be more empathy in her gestures now. "I'm no doctor, I have no idea. Maybe splicing in the insect DNA starts an incubation period."

"A period that ends when the host is twenty-five years old," I suggest.

Shannon collapses back into her chair, deflated. "Jesus fucking Christ."

"Your guess is as good as mine," says the woman in the beret.

"I'm with your friend," says another voice in the room. "Get it cut out of you. Then spread the word."

"If I get it cut out of me, they'll throw the thing away and no one will ever believe me."

"No one will believe you anyway," someone says.

"Unless the evidence is irrefutable," I mutter in response.

"We'll cover you," says someone else. "Let us write about you. Innocent victim of the sins of the past."

"A little on the nose, don't you think?" another voice asks.

"Good! Fuck subtlety," says the woman in the beret. "That's not what we need right now."

"I need to think about this," I say, with more resignation in my voice than I intend.

"Think about what, Darren?" Shannon asks. "Does your life mean this little to you?"

I shake my head again, robotically. "Actually, it's never meant as much as it does right now."

There's another long silence. The sky has turned purple with the dusk. I feel comforted, strangely, in this alien space—a space of fire and dedication, in which real change might happen. Can I be part of that? I've always thought of political action as a long, slow process, filled with meaningless tact, the calling of senators, marches that look good on social media, diatribes in the company of family members who still believe in the sanctity of the state. But there must be some way to commit *real* action in a way that people can't ignore.

Shannon insists on leaving—she needs some fresh air, she says. I tell her I need a minute, a few more questions need answering. She nearly sprints from the room and down the dirty, tiled stairs, then waits outside near a pair of double doors, next to a rank dumpster. I don't stay much longer, less than twenty minutes, but everything changes during that amount of time. I join a few of the women in another, smaller room, barely bigger than a janitor's closet, with hunks of outdated technology piled on metal shelves. The ringleader in the beret rifles through them, shoving aside computer monitors the size of cinder blocks and digital camcorders that were all the rage in the early nineties. Finally, we find what we're looking for: a small black case, no bigger than a shoebox, with a zipper running along the side. I clutch the case with a sweaty grip, pressing it against my side, hoping Shannon won't ask too many questions.

* * *

"Let me drive you to the hospital. *Now.*"

I half-expect Shannon to bind my hands and shove a gag in my mouth, then carry me in, kicking and flailing, to a doctor for my miraculous cure. We pass a hospital and two clinics on the way back to Fremont. Each time, Shannon glares at me and drifts toward the entrance. She makes empty threats: "If you don't let me take you in right now, I'm not helping you again. This is it. You can count me out." But her wavering voice betrays her uncertainty, her deeply wounded nature. Here's a person whose first thought is helping somebody else—a truly good person, that rarest breed. And I have the nerve to refuse her kindness.

"I can't do it, Shannon. I'm more tired than I've ever been. I need to go home."

She squints her eyes even tighter, somehow, and gives me a phlegmy cough.

"I think it's better, really—the physical stuff. I just need to think."

We drive another two minutes in silence. Finally, she relents and offers a gentle sigh.

"How 'bout a trade?" she asks gently. "I'll drop you at home tonight if you let me pick you up bright and early tomorrow—eight o'clock. Then we're going to see Dr. Carstens. No arguments."

I smile meekly. "No arguments." For the first time today, she offers me a smirk in return.

When she pulls up to the curb on Massachusetts Avenue, I ask her if she wants to come in. She raises her eyebrows in surprise, shifting the gear to park.

"You sure you're up for some company?"

There are countless things I want to say in response—things that can never really be expressed through words—but I can only offer a slight nod, which jars loose the tears welling in the corners of my eyes.

We step through the front door, Shannon slowing her movements so I can keep up with her. It's only seven o'clock—my mom has sent me a few texts and left me a voicemail, but I know she's working at Kibby's tonight, she won't be home until after midnight.

I collapse on the couch as soon as I can, needing to rest my mind and body. Shannon takes the long way around the sofa, her footsteps creaking the wooden boards. I've never felt one way or another about this house: it was a place to live, not pretty but functional, good enough for my undiscerning tastes. But gazing around the room now, feeling wetness in my eyes and all throughout my body, I've never loved it so much, its modest quirks and charms. There's a framed photo of a beachside cove that none of my family has ever visited; I used to think its out-of-placeness was absurd, but now I'm moved by its sense of longing, the possibility that *someday* we could go there. The old quilt thrown over the back of the sofa, the mostly warped records in my mom's collection, the hand-me-down lamps casting odd shadows from the end tables: how have I never seen how beautiful they are?

Before Shannon sits, I point at the record player and vinyl collection in the corner of the room. "Want to put on some music?" I mutter. She smiles, even though I can tell she doesn't particularly want to, and steps across the room and flips through the stack of LPs. After a minute or so, she pulls out some Fleetwood Mac, places it on the record player, and gingerly puts the needle in the groove as mellow sounds fill the room.

At last, Shannon returns to the couch, lifts my prostrate legs, and sits a few feet away, placing my sweat-dampened socks on her thighs. She can't help but give me a twisted grin as she does so. "Do you think you're contagious?"

I offer a guttural laugh. "For better or worse, I think it's hereditary."

We smile meekly but the levity fades. Shannon shakes her head before speaking again.

"Darren, I have no idea if what they said today is even remotely true. It all seems totally fucking absurd, but who knows? I don't want to tell you what's going on inside your body. But I'm pleading with you: take care of yourself."

I think, closing my eyes, listening to Stevie Nicks' pained voice. "I don't even know how to do that."

She's ready to respond with a torrent of invective, but instead she closes her mouth, looks at a distant corner of the ceiling, and takes a deep breath. "You promise me you'll see the doctor tomorrow?" I say nothing. "I can't stand the thought of you . . . giving up."

I shake my head as vigorously as my weakened state allows. "I'm not giving up. I finally have a plan. But yes, I promise." I swallow roughly, hoping my words sound convincing. "I'll see the doctor tomorrow."

After a few hours of dormancy, the intruder inside me wakes up with a roar, as if angered by the words I've spoken. There's an unbearable pain in my gut, a shockwave rising and falling at once. Out of the corner of my eye, I see it: a huge protuberance poking out of my gut, now nearly the size of a baseball, straining against the fabric of my shirt. Shannon sees it too, a throbbing shape straining against the borders of my body. She throws my feet off her and stands with a jolt, unable to suppress a scream.

I wobble to my feet and make a beeline for the bathroom, Shannon trailing behind me and holding my arm for support. I shrug off her help as I reach the bathroom door, close it behind me, collapse in front of the toilet, and vomit again. It's less red this time, less deep crimson, which should be reassuring but there's something else instead: a thick slime, oozing from my body, like nothing I've ever seen before. As I watch it droop into the toilet bowl, I can think only of the viscous mess that results when you step on an unsuspecting bug and lift your boot—a prehistoric slime, not quite clear, flecked with white.

Shannon offers reassurances through the door, her voice uneasy. She gets me a glass of water and toasts two pieces of bread, then covers them lightly with butter, sliding them through the door as she cracks it open. When I emerge from the bathroom a few minutes later, too scared and tired to be embarrassed, she ushers me to my bedroom and helps me into bed, tucking a thin comforter under my chin. I'm shivering, aflame and freezing at once, and I realize whatever superhuman abilities this experiment was meant to manifest are nowhere in sight. I also realize I'm undeserving of Shannon's generosity, which is wasted on a doomed man like me.

I raise my eyes to see Shannon's look of nausea as she sits at the end of the bed, giving me space.

"Sure I can't take you anywhere now?"

I shake my head and close my eyes. "Tomorrow morning."

"Okay. Tomorrow morning." She runs a hand along my sweaty brow. "You promised."

"Tomorrow morning."

There's a long pause. The sound of birds and laughter outside—I don't know if it's comforting or spiteful.

"I should go. Let you get some rest."

I look into her eyes. I can tell by her reaction that my own eyes have become even more bloodshot, striped with red and yellow, growing inhuman.

"Shannon. Thank you, for everything. I wish we could have done this a while ago. Before . . ."

She smiles sadly. I see tears in her eyes.

"We'll do it right soon. A couple weeks, next month, whenever. When you're feeling healthy again."

There's a lot I want to say in response, but I've learned my lesson: I can't betray her trust, not now.

"I want to get to know you better," I moan.

"Me too. One thing's for sure, Darren, you're a mystery. I feel like if I know you for the next fifty years, I still won't understand you."

I reach out my hand to hers. She holds it close. It nearly slips from her grip, frail and coated with sweat.

"I wish that could happen . . ."

My words start slurring before I finish my thought, and I drift off to sleep. I think I hear Shannon asking me what I mean before the world grows black.

* * *

I will never remember the dreams I have over the next six hours, but they're the strangest nightmares I've ever known, millennia old and inherited from other species. Scuttling over an arid desert floor, the ground breaks up before me, great tectonic plates separating and lifting, opening a deep purple void between them. Someone is swimming in the miasma between the land masses. It's my parents, my mother and father, looking blissful. I lurch over the side of my patch of desert and hurtle toward them, floating in zero gravity. Nearly upon them now, I see they're not humans at all, but rather ancient insects with thousands of legs and big, fat thoraxes pulsing with juices struggling to break free. There are other insects beyond them, an infinite array of squirming legs and twitching antennae. This battalion goes on into the distance, creating a slimy entomological landscape that defines the entire universe.

* * *

I wake at one-thirty with the sound of a car door slamming, the jingle of keys and the quiet opening of the front door. Mom is home after another seventeen-hour day. My ears track her movements through the rooms: dropping keys and purse on the end table, kicking off shoes en route to the kitchen, opening up the fridge and prying off a Corona bottlecap, rummaging for leftovers or whatever's easiest to make for a late-night dinner.

I'm still deathly tired, but I kick the blankets off me and swing my legs over the side of the bed. I stumble out of my room, down the short hallway and to the left, toward the kitchen. I think about stopping off in the bathroom before I do, but seeing my reflection is a dismal shock I don't need right now.

In any case, I know my appearance as soon as my mom looks up from her position at the small, round table. She wears exhaustion as though it's a fashionable accoutrement, but throws it off abruptly as she spots me lurking in the arched doorway. She rises to her feet, the chair sliding across the floor, and crosses the room in large, anxious steps.

"Jesus, Darren." She squints at me, cradling my face in both her hands. "Honey. Honey. You look terrible."

"I know."

"Why didn't you *tell* me it was this bad?" I can see self-reproach finding its way into her expression, mixed with the maelstrom of emotions she habitually hides. "I'm not a prisoner at work, you know. I can come home for you."

"There's nothing you could do. I just needed to rest."

"The doctor. Tomorrow. Okay? I'm taking you."

I sigh and lean against the wall. "My friend is taking me tomorrow morning. It's okay."

"Your friend? Darren . . . I'm your *mother*. I can take you."

"Don't you have work?"

She exhales loudly. "Do I have work. Work. Godforsaken work." She gives me an apologetic smile. "Sorry. I'll take off. I can do that, you know. I'm going with you."

A pang of nervousness strikes me all of a sudden, for approximately a million reasons. "She's taking me at eight. They'll just run some tests, you know? Maybe you could come by on your lunch break? Or see me at home afterwards."

She shakes her head again, a movement that sums up her entire worldview. "Are you sure? I mean, they'll understand. They fired Frances after she didn't show up for her shift this week. But this is important. They'll understand. I've been there twelve years, they goddamn better understand." She frowns at me, trying to play it off as humorous. "Why am I telling you this? Sorry, just tired. Yes! Of course I can go with you tomorrow morning, Darren."

"Do you mind if I sit down?" I gesture at the seat across from hers at the table.

"Of course not, honey. Honey. Sit down." She pulls the chair out for me. Her water on the stove is boiling. She pours in some spaghetti noodles and glops some marinara into a second saucepan—whatever was the cheapest sauce they had at the store. "*She?* Your friend, this *she . . .* anyone I should know about?"

I smile darkly, sadly. "No. Not yet."

She sits across from me and takes a tired swig of Corona. "Okay, if you say so. Is it still this . . . stomach issue?"

I nod. Then steel myself for a difficult conversation at almost two in the morning. "Yeah. A day away from my birthday. Just like Dad."

I expect her to respond with fury and defensiveness. Instead, she stares resolutely at the label on her beer bottle. Then chokes herself into a debilitating sob, the tears flowing out in a torrent. She covers her mouth with her forearm, shuts her eyes tight, looks in every direction except at me. This happens for another few seconds until I get up, lurch to the seat on her left, and place a wet, feverish hand on her shoulder.

"I went to the VA hospital. Talked to Dr. Sharp. Remember him?"

She looks at me and laughs in spite of herself. "He's still there?"

"And he remembers Dad. I pissed him off all over again."

"Good." She smiles and wipes away a few more tears. "Good."

I move my hand from her shoulder to her thin, narrow wrist. "He told me what happened. The army coming in, stopping the surgery. Giving you some neat and tidy bullshit explanation."

We both sit there, not knowing what to say. The sound of sauce and water boiling rises to a deafening pitch. My mother stands, empties the noodles into a strainer, tastes the sauce, empties both into a bowl, then stands, palms extended against the counter, for minutes on end.

"You must hate me," she says at last.

"No. No." I stand, move to her, and hug her from behind. "I think I know you better than I ever have."

She squeezes my forearm gently but continues looking in the other direction. "I don't understand. We tested you as soon as you were born. Every test we could possibly think of. You were a healthy, normal, *beautiful* boy."

I take a long time to respond. "I think whatever's happening to me—what happened to Dad—it's not, like, a medical thing."

She turns around. Wipes more tears from the protruding bags beneath her eyes. I don't know how she does it. The majority of each day spent as a worker. No time, except for the weekends, to devote to herself, to retain her humanity. And even then, errands: the bank, the grocery store, the post office, the hardware store. The only upside, I guess, is that it leaves her little time to think about everything else.

"What do you mean?" she asks.

"You know what I mean. He stayed overseas for two years after the end of the war. Don't you think something happened then?"

She holds my face in both her hands again, gazing into my hazel eyes. "Honey. Maybe. Yeah, I guess so."

"And they never told you what. Never compensated you for losing him. Never . . . they never cared."

She nods, looks down at the floor, then moves away from me, grabs her bowl of pasta, and returns to the table. I follow after her, sitting close to her left. I can only stare at the cheap plastic surface of the table, made to look like rustic wood.

"Sorry, I'm ravenous. I need to eat." She devours a couple forkfuls of pasta. I can only watch her, relishing every move-ment, studying her as if my observations must last for posterity. "What you're talking about," she says between overfull bites, "army experiments, unexplained deaths. These things don't happen. Not to regular people."

I can't help but laugh. "What does that mean? Anyway, Mom . . . I think it's too late to pretend otherwise."

She throws her fork down in her bowl, adamant. "Not too late. Not too late for you. We're going to the doctor tomorrow.

Okay?"

I smile and nod again. "I told you, I'm going. My friend is taking me. But I'm not waking up at the asscrack of dawn like you." We both laugh, a forced, inhuman sound. "But it'll be fine. I'll get looked at and you can see me afterward."

She leans forward on both her elbows, taking in my haggard appearance. I wonder why we haven't had a conversation like this in—what, ten years?

"How did I . . ." She trails off, takes another bite of pasta, staring at the red conflagration in her bowl. "There are a lot of things I don't say to you that I probably should."

"Me too. I didn't think I had to, until I started worrying about—time, I guess."

She looks up at me again. "Don't say that."

"Why not? I wish I worried about it earlier."

She takes another swig of Corona, finishing her first beer. "You know what I think is one of the worst things I've done? Pretending to be happy all the time. 'It's fine, it'll be okay.' Convincing myself that Bryan would be okay, it was just a little stomach bug, he'd get over it. Convincing myself that you were fine too, despite what happened to him—that's some epic self-delusion, don't you think? Convincing myself that I can go on working two jobs, every day, and eventually we'd have enough to live on. Convincing myself you and me would be able to get closer, someday, when things settle down. Buck up, be happy, work hard, it'll be alright. If you say that to yourself enough times, you know what? You start to believe it. Start to be content with unhappiness. And that's a bad way to live."

"You've given me more than enough, Mom. I've had a good life."

"Don't say it like that!"

"I have. That's all I wanted to say. I see everything you do for me."

"Don't say it like everything is so *final*, Darren."

"I don't know if it's final, but I need to say it. And I want you to live your own life. That happiness doesn't have to be fake, you know."

She smiles, shakes her head, finishes her bowl of pasta. Then reaches behind her and plucks another Corona from the fridge without getting up.

"You sound like my dad," she says. "Isn't it supposed to be the other way around?"

I smile, happy for a moment. There's an earthquake pain in the center of my gut, but I shut it out of mind, not willing to deal with it currently.

"Doesn't matter, Mom. We got each other."

I stand, move behind her chair. Kiss the top of her head, which smells like Corona, cigarette smoke, spearmint gum, and cheap perfume. If that's the last scent on Earth I experience, I'll be content.

Friday

I wake at seven with a thunderous pain that feels like a godsend. This stranger, this parasite, this blob of disease, it's become a soul mate I feel I've always known.

I walk, calmly and patiently, to the bathroom, where I kneel and spew a geyser of blood into the welcoming porcelain god. Unable to resist my morbid curiosity, I lift my sweaty gray T-shirt and stare down at my abdomen. There's a black-purple bruise that looks like overripe currants, about the size of a fist in the middle of my gut; underneath it, something squirms and fidgets, sending ripples across my skin that remind me of a wading pool, throbbing pain notwithstanding.

Shannon arrives thirty minutes later, red Honda pulling up to the curb. I've been waiting outside in the interim, basking in the warmth of the sun, its golden brilliance. Its heat doesn't bother me anymore. I watch an old man struggle to the corner to wait for the bus, and I feel like I know him better than I've known anyone before, comprehending his hopes and dreams with each flimsy step. I watch an army of ants work in unison as they carry a small twig down the sidewalk, admiring their unspoken communication. I watch a cardinal soar to its nest in the trees and offer something to its offspring. Every sight grants me deep, fulfilling pleasure—all is right with the world.

Shannon gets out and helps me into the car, ushering me down the sidewalk and onto the passenger seat as though I'm three times my age, riddled with defects. There's none of her anger from the previous day, as she thinks she's driving me to my salvation.

When we arrive at Priority Care Clinics to the west of the city, Shannon parks and walks me to the front entrance. We approach the front desk and ask if Dr. Carstens is available for an urgent appointment. She's busy, the receptionist says, but should be free in about an hour; if my situation is life-threatening, she adds, other doctors are available. Before Shannon can respond, I assure her it's no hurry, and we take a seat in the waiting room. I grab an issue of *Entertainment Weekly*. The latest Marvel movie is set for release, the magazine says, and I know it will be exactly the same as all the others.

The pain continues to fester in my body, and I have to rush to the bathroom several times. I wear a loose-fitting white dress shirt in anticipation of this issue, and I carry a blue sport coat with me in case I need to conceal any physiological horrors. (Shannon raised her eyes when she first saw me this morning, struck by my unusually professional appearance. "At least I can *try* to make myself look good," I told her—concealing the real reason for my semblance of dignity.)

During one venture to the bathroom, with Shannon gently placing her hand against my back and guiding me along, I lift up my shirt and take another look at my parasite, Gregor. He's growing increasingly restless, like a toddler throwing a temper tantrum. His contours are now clear to me: an oval shape for the head, the thorax, and the abdomen, squirming in restless formations. His antennae tickling my interior, tiny dots pressing against the skin. His spiracles switching position with his head and scraping against my bowels, somersaulting. Now, when he's almost fully formed, I have an idea of the grace and beauty of this animal. Add pride to the mix of nonsensical emotions flooding my hijacked brain.

The long wait has a benefit. It's nearly eleven o'clock and Shannon is getting restless. Still no word from Dr. Carstens, who is busy with other patients.

"You've skipped a couple days of work," I say as casually as possible.

"For which I owe you many thanks."

"You're welcome to use me as an excuse. But Charlie is probably getting mad." I smirk as I envision our crotchety supervisor, who always finds something to complain about despite the decidedly low stakes of our place of employment.

Shannon shrugs but stares at thin carpet, pondering how this will affect her paycheck.

"Listen," I tell her cheerfully. "I'll be here for hours. There's nothing you can do. I'm sure they'll give me tests, maybe surgery, whatever. Just see me after work. I'll keep you posted."

She gazes at me, her look guilty but appreciative. "You sure?"

"You've done more than enough. I mean that—more than anybody would do. Go make some money and I'll see you later. Okay?"

She smiles and kisses me on the cheek; the sensation thrills me, though it must be unpleasant for her, lips grazing a layer of sweat. Then she stands and peers down at me.

"After you get better, I expect the best first date a girl has ever been on."

"Was this not a first date?"

She laughs, then moves in the other direction. I ignore the pain, stand, and follow after her, then grab her hand lightly and spin her around. I wrap my arms around her and pull her close. I hope she doesn't mind our prolonged contact.

"For however long I know you, I think I really like you." I swallow, then speak again. "Love you."

She pulls away, looks at me. There's no smile, no frown. A deep and solemn inquisitiveness.

"I think I really like you love you too. And I'll know you a long time."

I smile. *No tears*, I say to myself, and I'm able to keep them withheld.

"I hope so."

She scratches the back of her hand against my unshaven cheek, and that's the last human touch I'll ever enjoy.

* * *

I send a text to my mom:

Still waiting for the doctor. I'll let you know soon.

Then send a digital postscript:

Love you. Thanks for everything.

It's been more than three hours and still no word from Dr. Carstens or the admitting clerk at the front desk. Normally, such an interminable wait in the face of severe distress would have me railing against the cruelty of our healthcare system. But today, the long wait is exactly what I'd hoped for: an opportunity to mobilize.

I straighten my dress shirt, then hobble to my feet, steady myself, and shuffle through the waiting room to the bathroom. The lights overhead are violent and abrasive, and I wonder if I'm seeing them differently, through arthropod eyes.

I lurch into a bathroom stall and close the salmon-colored

door, latching it carefully. From beneath my shirt I retrieve the small black case that the revolutionaries at *The Equator* gave me yesterday. I unzip the case and place it on the closed toilet, revealing an array of tiny technological equipment. There's a pair of eyeglasses with thick black rims and a microphone that's nearly microscopic. Embedded in the frame of the glasses is a camera no bigger than the tip of a pencil. I put on the glasses, feeling them slide across my slick skin and through my curly black hair, which I haven't washed in days. I feel the upper right corner of the glasses; there's a minuscule plastic nib that makes contact with my index finger, and I push it down until I see a faint blue light pulse in my peripheral vision. Then, finally, I lift the microphone from the black felt case; it looks more like a microchip that you'd find inside your phone. The equipment is so minuscule that a small jolt of pressure could crush it. I slide my middle finger under it and lift it carefully; the underside has an adhesive surface that attaches to nearly any fabric. I press the chip against the inside of my shirt collar, only a few inches away from my lips. The chip contains not only a microphone, but also a transmitter that relays sounds to satellites thirteen thousand miles away. The images only go so far as a relay antenna about ten miles away in Dundalk, but from there they can be sent nearly anywhere in the world.

Now fully outfitted for my self-imposed mission, I throw on my sport coat, adjust my clothes, and pat the sycophant within me. "Alright, Gregor. I think you're driving me crazy. But it seems we have something important to do. Are you with me?" The little thing kicks at my insides. There's another tsunami of pain, but somehow this most recent agitation feels almost loving. I'm reminded, absurdly, of a high school football coach giving his lackluster players a pep talk—an experience I had only my last year of middle school, before quitting organized sports soon after. But I'm enjoying my performance and, squatting slightly, yell in the direction of my navel: "I said are you with me?!"

Halfway through this final bellow, someone enters the bathroom and approaches the urinals. I bolt from the bathroom stall, wash my hands, and skid back into the clinic waiting room, adamantly avoiding the dubious stare of the man who interrupted my motivational speech.

But instead of taking my seat once again, I walk as quickly as my gelatin legs will carry me across the lobby, toward the sliding doors at the entrance. As I drag my body out of the building, I think I hear the front desk clerk finally calling my name, as Dr. Carstens has apparently become free. But it's too late, I think, in countless ways; my decision has been made. Sure, I could stop and see Dr. Carstens and maybe then everything would end okay. But I've been offered something greater.

The summer air greets me with a symphony of light and sound, more majestic than it's ever seemed before. I don't even mind the long voyage that awaits me—I only hope my body (and little Gregor) cooperate.

As I wait for the bus that will take me to the MARC station in Halethorpe, I make a call to the woman in the beret I met in Dundalk yesterday. Leila is her name, she told me proudly—named after Leila Abouzeid, one of the best-known authors from her homeland. She's awaiting my call. I tell her the equipment is ready to go. In curt but supportive tones, she tells me that she already knows: she can see shaky but crystal-clear images from my woozy walk to the bus stop. She can also hear the sounds of southwest Baltimore, patched in separately but synced with the video track. I can picture the bank of video monitors and small, decrepit speakers that were set up in their compound the previous day. She tells me *The Equator* has not only emailed its followers, but also contacted journalists in Baltimore and posted messages in activist groups throughout the country. "We have about fifty people in the waiting room already," she says, referring to the online network through which my ordeal will be broadcast. "More joining every second." I know the livestream won't begin for a few hours. *Stage fright* hardly seems like an appropriate epithet for what awaits me. "Just do what you set out to do," she breathes across the phone. "We'll take care of everything else."

The bus arrives thirty seconds later. I've memorized the route from Baltimore to Fort Detrick, poring over the steps countless times. I take the MARC train to the airport, then the Gaithersburg train to Shady Grove station. After a quick transfer in Redland, I continue on the train to Monocacy station, which is near Ballenger Creek on the outskirts of Frederick. Then it's only a quick ride to Fort Detrick, an expanse of unassuming white buildings, outside of which the armed guards with rapid-fire assault rifles don't make themselves known until you're right in front of them.

The journey takes almost four hours, all of it on bus and train. My body mostly obeys, despite a couple desperate trips to the claustrophobic train restroom. It's as though some kind of synchronicity has developed between me and my progeny: Gregor knows we have a destination in mind and refuses to cause too much of a fuss. I can't explain it: I feel a morbid kind of love for this thing growing inside me. For the first time ever, I feel my life has direction.

The long expedition gives me time to think. There's the inevitable guilt and shame for lying to Shannon and my mother, provoked by text messages and voicemails from both of them—if all goes as I expect, I'll never speak to them again. I want to return the love they've given me, embrace a long and happy life. But this feels like something unattainable. Has the specter of my father convinced me? Or is it the influence of Gregor inside me, driving me closer to its liberation—and my own extermination? I don't know where it comes from, but I know where I'm going. There's no way I could explain this to Shannon, to my mom, to the people I love the most. And it makes me feel monstrous as I seek my self-destruction, though I have no doubts about the path that awaits me.

What is the value of martyrdom? That word has seemed antiquated for at least a few centuries; death is so rampant that martyrs are an extinct brccd, a fact of pandemic life, not something to be lionized. But is there something noble about death with purpose? There was the climate activist who immolated himself in front of the Supreme Court, urging, forcing, demanding people to recognize that their lives on this planet are not guaranteed. (His name bubbles from the depths of my subconscious: Wynn Bruce. A martyr.) If his death had gotten more publicity, it might have made an impact. But no, his name and agenda were overshadowed by Trump, Putin, rising gas prices. If you want to make yourself heard, even setting yourself on fire isn't loud enough.

A lofty comparison, maybe. I didn't want to be a martyr. For years, I thought my life's purpose was to watch movies, read books, fuck around, avoid the difficulties of existence. A microscopic speck a few light years away in the cosmos doesn't care about me—why should I take myself too seriously among such vastness? Of course, I thought so before some cockroach was spawned inside my stomach, a legacy of my father's duty to his country. But these overblown philosophies of mine don't take into account the people I love. A few years ago, the meaning of that ubiquitous word, *love*, would never have occurred to me; there are simply people inside and outside your orbit, going through their everyday lives. That's what I used to think, anyway. More than anything else, the callous way that I used to live is what gives me shame. Love is the thing that makes us human and I've never taken it seriously.

* * *

I arrive in Frederick around half past three, the Monocacy train station a modest brick building with an open platform and quaint, flowering trees. Here in the suburbs, there are a few other commuters heading home after work, seeking out their luxury sedans and SUVs in the nearby parking lot. I find refuge on a bench and order a Lyft to take me to Fort Detrick. It's only about a fifteen-minute ride; the driver who picks me up in a white Toyota Highlander is named Saddiq and offers little conversation as we drive through Frederick. I take in its gorgeous downtown district and stately homes, most of which are purchased through military wealth—surface beauty propped up by an ignoble history.

Visitors at Fort Detrick are funneled through the Nallin Farm Gate to the Visitor Center, which looks innocuous enough, flanked by ponds and a tranquil park across the street. There's a community college next door, and I wonder if the students know that they'd be the first to go if the biological agents housed at the fort were somehow unleashed.

I pay Saddiq as he drops me off at the Visitor Center, then lurch inside, watching the SUV drive away. If this harebrained plot somehow doesn't work out, I think, I'll be stranded here—forced to depend on the love of Shannon or my mother once again.

Most military forts—at least the outward-facing aspects that the public usually sees—are meant to look like quotidian office buildings, with gleaming tile lobbies, polite front desk clerks, and sunlight pouring in through well-placed skylights. I hobble up to one of the clerks, checking that my shirt and coat are smooth and dignified, and straighten the glasses on my face, which I hope looks toned instead of haggard. There's a rumble inside my gut, not quite excruciating, as though my little parasite has perked up inside me, eager to see where this caper goes.

"Hello," offers the silky female voice that greets me. She wears a tight ponytail and subtle but immaculate makeup. If she has any reservations about my dismal appearance, she hides them well.

"Hi. I'm here to see an officer—Colonel Tim Stocker."

"Oh, he would be in our military personnel division. That's about a mile down Campus Drive. Do you have an appointment?"

"No. I'm a friend of the family. To be honest, I was hoping to surprise him."

She squints, her eyebrows furrowed in distrust. I don't blame her.

"I doubt you'll be able to see him today. He might already be gone . . ."

"Can you call his office, please? My name is Darren Trevor. Please tell him I'm here—he'll recognize the name. My dad was Bryan Trevor."

She sighs, shakes her head slightly. I clear my throat and lean in closer.

"Please. I've come a long way. The colonel will be glad to see me."

Recognizing that I won't give up easily, she lifts a phone off its cradle and punches some numbers. Then she rests the phone between her shoulder and neck, propping the receiver against her head. It rings a few times. I stare directly at her, not realizing I'm doing so. Finally, someone answers.

"Hi, Darlene?" says the woman in front of me. "I have someone here who wants to see Colonel Stocker." A pause as Darlene responds on the other end of the line. "No, I know. He doesn't have an appointment." Another pause. The desk attendant lifts her eyes in my direction. "What is this about, exactly?"

"He knows my father, Bryan Trevor. He was my dad's CO back in the Gulf War. I've never met the colonel, but he and my dad were close. I think he'd like to meet me."

The woman speaks into the mouthpiece again. "Says his dad is Bryan Trevor—one of his soldiers in Iraq a long time ago." She looks up at me. "What was your name again?"

"Darren."

"Darren," she says into the phone.

The next pause takes an eternity—another imperial war could be fought in the interim. I feign a casual appearance, glancing around the expansive lobby, but really my mind is racing with a million chaotic thoughts. Life, finality, war, hope, cruelty, glory, sacrifice, loss—not enough time to consider any one concept with any complexity. I wonder, too, how many people are logged into the livestream now—is my and Gregor's current performance available for all to see? Finally, I wonder how much it will hurt, my unique moment of birth and death. The pain continues to rise inside of me, but at least it's a dull throb; I think the constant pressure against the inside of my gut will be tolerable, at least until the moment of revelation.

Finally, the desk attendant looks up at me, unable to conceal her surprise.

"He'll see you. Just drive straight down Campus," she says, nodding her head in the other direction over her shoulder, "and you'll run right into the personnel center. You'll need to be checked in there."

"I don't have a car."

"You don't?"

I shake my head.

"I'll get someone to drive you."

I wait in front of the building until a gleaming black Range Rover pulls up, a trio of soldiers in camo gear, each carrying gargantuan assault rifles, pouring out in unison.

"Darren Trevor." He says it as a statement, not a question. I nod. Another of the soldiers steps up to pat me down with force, spreading my legs and lifting my arms, swatting at my clothing, running his hand through my hair, inspecting my phone and my wallet. The third soldier has his gun trained on me the entire time. Luckily, they don't examine my body for any internal stowaways with gruesome intent.

Placated at last, they shove me into the open rear door of the Range Rover and pile in after me. The vehicle screeches away from the Visitor Center, peeling down the road and arriving at the Personnel Division in less than a minute.

The inquisition continues at this building: I'm prodded inside, then ushered through a metal detector, where all of my accessories (glasses, wallet, phone, shoes) are inspected carefully by a man in a too-tight uniform. I hold my breath as he fondles the glasses in his palm, inspecting them closely; but he's finally satisfied, placing everything in a plastic tray and sliding it to the end of the metal detector.

The soldier who said my name outside the Visitor Center speaks again: "Follow me." Without a moment's pause, he pivots on his polished black boots, flitting down the narrow hallway. We come to the end, then take a sharp left to a bank of elevators. Behind closed doors, the sounds of hushed phone conversations and business meetings can be heard; if I didn't know any better, this could be the most top-secret office supply company in the world.

We venture up to the third floor, snaking down hallways, until we arrive at room 317: Colonel Timothy Stocker's office. Before I enter, the soldier orders me to check in with the assistant and reminds me the office is under surveillance.

"Thanks," I mutter before I walk in. Nonplussed, he twists away from me, nearly grazing my chest with the muzzle of his rifle.

After only about three minutes of waiting (on plush, burgundy-colored seats, his assistant eyeing me cagily the whole time), Colonel Stocker emerges from his office, an image of cliched military authority: muscular build, close-cropped hair graying at the temples, well-tanned, cocksure and brusque. He comes to a stop only one step outside his interior office, then offers a curt, obligatory smile.

"Mr. Trevor."

I stand woozily and walk toward him as confidently as I can. His expression can't hide a trace of revulsion at my gaunt and wizened appearance, but I imagine he feels compelled to show sympathy toward the son of a man he trained and (indirectly, I presume) killed.

"Colonel. Thank you for seeing me."

I hold out my hand for him to shake, not quite sure of the etiquette. He grasps my hand between both of his, crushing it so hard I almost feel the metacarpals break.

"I have an unwritten rule. Whenever the sons or daughters of my soldiers arrive at my doorstep, I welcome them with open arms. Nothing's more important than the power of lineage."

I nod uncertainly.

"Please. Come in."

He rotates on the balls of his feet—a motion I'm sure has been bred into his very being. I follow him into his office. It's a plush, ostentatious room, the habitat of a man who's been rewarded for his decades of service. There's a long, rosewood desk to our left, almost reddish in color, which I imagine weighs more than a ton and can never leave this building again. The colonel sidesteps the desk, falling gracefully into an expensive-looking chair with green backing; it jostles on its wheels before settling into place. I take one of two stationary chairs on the other side, which are upholstered in the same green color. Behind Stocker, there's a vast and spotless window, though the view is hardly impressive: a muddy field with rectangular buildings in the distance. A framed portrait of President Biden is hung on the wall behind him, over his right shoulder. Over his left, a barrage of framed photos and commendations: medals, certificates, portraits with Trump, both Clintons, Cheney, Obama, Macron, Merkel, the Saudi prime minister Salman, the Egyptian president Fattah el-Sisi, Xi Jinping, Bolsonaro, a veritable roster of international heads of state. On his desk, a marble paperweight of a noble bald eagle. To the right of me when I sit down, an American flag extends from a base on the floor. I've never felt so out of place.

"So. You're Bryan Trevor's son. Darren, right?"

"That's right."

"I gotta tell you. I haven't heard that name in years. Decades. A lot of feelings came back when I heard the name Bryan Trevor."

"What kind of feelings?"

He shrugs. If he's suspicious of me at all, he won't allow such anxieties to show themselves. There's only firm, untouchable conviction.

"Pride. Most of all, pride. I met him when he was only eighteen. Did you know that? Just a kid. He became a man before my very eyes."

"You were his CO in Iraq, right?"

I swallow the last word. There's a ferocious stabbing in my gut, a newly emphatic outburst from the thing inside me. I glance down at my white dress shirt and see a momentary bulge, like one of those whack-a-mole games. There's even a trickling of blood, the inside breaking out, making itself visible. My eyes dart upward; apparently, the colonel hasn't noticed.

"That's right. It was a quick war because of men like him. Brave, dutiful, self-sacrificing. He believed in something greater than himself, which you can't say about a lot of men anymore."

"And Saudi Arabia, too? I read my dad's records the other day. Rafha, Basra, and Amarah, I think it said."

"That's right. The whole 1/18 was stationed there. Some of the greatest men I ever knew."

"What else did you feel? When you heard his name, I mean."

Stocker raises his eyes toward the ceiling, contemplating the question, or at least pretending to. "Sorrow. Regret. I know we lost him too soon. Am I right about that, son?"

"Yeah, you're right. I never knew him."

"I'm sorry to hear that. I thought that might be the case. But I was hoping it wasn't. Really, though, what I felt most of all was love. A lot of men in my position won't say that—but most of them feel it. Love for the men they lead."

"I appreciate you saying that."

"It's the truth. That's why I say it."

"Where else did he serve under you?"

"What do you mean? Nowhere else."

"Really? I'm just asking, I don't know, I was confused. Ground combat ended in '91, right? But he came back in '93. I was curious what he did during that time."

"That's what you heard?"

"That's what the records say. Not a lot more than that. But, yeah—he was gone from '91 to February of '93. If he was there for the war, that's, what . . . almost two years unaccounted for?"

"Well, it's not as simple as what you read on Wikipedia. Military retreats aren't instantaneous."

"Hmm." My hyperbolic sigh is a bad idea: it provokes another kick from Gregor, another spurt of blood running along the buttons that bisect my shirt. I drag my feet against the floor and push my chair closer to the desk, hoping the colonel doesn't see the bloody evidence.

"As for what he did after the war," Stocker continues, "it could be any number of things. There were a lot of private contractors in the Middle East around that time—not as many as after the Iraq War or Inherent Resolve, but still."

"Or Operation Echidna?"

For the first time, Colonel Stocker balks, retreating backwards in his chair a fraction of an inch. His eyes narrow infinitesimally beneath thick brows. He collects himself before he answers.

"I have no idea what that is."

"I think you do. I know you do."

"You *know* . . ." He reconsiders this train of thought, breathes, starts again. "Why did you come here today, son?"

"There's a lot I don't know. I mean, I never met my dad. So I'm just trying to get some answers."

He frowns. "I appreciate that. My time with your father was brief. I knew him during the war, and he was a great man. Loyal, courageous. What happened to him afterwards, I'm sorry to say, I don't really know."

"That's not true. You led Operation Echidna. An experiment, right? Infusing soldiers' DNA with that of insects. *Cockroaches*." I say the last word with emphatic spite, and Gregor scrapes against my abdominal wall again. "Turn them into . . ."

"*Infuse* them with insect DNA?"

". . . ultimate killing machines. Even if they die in the process. 'Cuz they're expendable, isn't that what you think?"

"Son," the colonel growls while shaking his head, "conspiracy theories can be dangerous. And this is the most fucked-up conspiracy theory I've heard in ages, excuse my language."

"There are records. You know that? Classified documents, which aren't as hard to find as you might think."

"Documents can be fabricated. I think you're the victim of a—"

The sound of a great ripping and a gurgling mess interrupt his response. I can't help but kick my feet against the carpet, pushing my chair back nearly a foot. I look down at my shirt. The lower half is now a crimson expanse, thick and heavy with blood. I felt it before I saw it—felt a sudden rupture in the borders of my body, which I thought had been impermeable.

"Jesus, what is this?" The look of fear on Stocker's face

is obvious. Which, to me, doesn't mean this result was unexpected.

There's another splitting, a rupture. The pain truly is unbearable this time, a massive fist punching my body from the inside out. A red gush sprays from somewhere inside me, over his desk, over the chair, over my shaking hands.

"I'm calling security."

He picks up the phone from his desk, as if that will do anything. But he never makes it as far as calling down to the front desk, or even to his assistant.

I spot a single, black, stiff antenna reaching out through my bloodstained shirt; the antenna meets the open air of the office and twitches in response.

In Dundalk, Leila and her colleagues watch on a grainy screen, a POV close-up of an insect being birthed into the world.

In Colonel Stocker's office, I breathe out a few more words: "You did this to him . . . you did this to him . . ."

On computers and phones in Baltimore and throughout the country, Southeast to Midwest to desert to Pacific, those who got the invite now witness the great expurgation. Coffee is spit upon digital screens, some vomit against their will, others cover their mouths as they retch, witnessing the carnage.

Stocker stands and recoils, leaning against the glass window. I savor his revulsion and bask in the gore.

One final thrust from the creature within me. A volcanic burst, an act of war. The pain is too much, I kick against the desk, sending the chair plummeting over backwards. I need to see it, I rip my shirt apart, buttons and flesh and blood splattering.

A fountain of blood sprays over the stars and stripes to the right of me, turning the flag a deep red.

My flesh tears further, further, further, until an insect the size of a grapefruit crawls out of it, its black beady eyes looking in every direction until they meet my own. Beautiful cockroach eyes, my birthright. In my last conscious moment, I peer into its soul and it peers into mine with love, understanding, and violence. The father, the offspring, I never knew.

www.ingramcontent.com/pod-product-compliance
Lightning Source LLC
Chambersburg PA
CBHW021021160726

47994CB00006B/2607